# INCIDENT AT CHRISTIVA

## *WELCOME TO THE GREY ZONE...*

...And its nefarious and shadowy landscape that knows no international borders.

...Whose each and every individual has special expertise, but no permanent ties or allegiances to any nationalities, countries, or governments. If you want a landmark statue shattered in New York City, a bridge blown in London, a tower toppled in Paris—but don't want any evidence left around to tie you to the crimes— you'll find people in the GREY ZONE who'll sign on to accomplish any and all of that—for a price!

Arms dealer Kel Meyers and his go-between, Jack York, are among those in the GREY ZONE who are involved in, or soon will be involved in, the *INCIDENT AT CHRISTIVA...*

## Borgo Press Books by WILLIAM MALTESE

# INCIDENT AT CHRISTIVA

## AN ESPIONAGE NOVEL: SPIES & LIES, BOOK THREE

## WILLIAM MALTESE

THE BORGO PRESS

MMXIII

# INCIDENT AT CHRISTIVA

FIRST EDITION

Published by Wildside Press LLC

www.wildsidebooks.com

# DEDICATION

To all those who have been there, done that,
got the t-shirt, burned it, and tossed the ashes.

# CONTENTS

# PROLOGUE

The sniper fired.

There was a dull thud as the resulting .30-06 caliber bullet passed through the uniform's camouflage cotton and into the muscular chesta beneath. The recipient's eyes registered glassy shock at unexpected death even as the impact of the slug repelled him backward into a bank of damp, rain-soaked earth. His rifle, the same German G3 as those of his compatriots who immediately returned fire, clattered to the ground, soon rediscovered by the lifeless corpse that slipped along wet grass to join it.

Jack York knew the dead man who, after all, had fought beside him for the past six month. He suspected the weapon that killed him was a U.S. M1903A4 sniper rifle. All the guns involved, the sniper's and otherwise, weren't newly manufactured but recycled from other wars, some of those ongoing conflicts begun and ended before this one even started. Recycled weaponry was not only still functional but cheaper than new. Although Dictator Stefano Peletto had lucked upon a new income source, with the discovery of a rare deposit of corolundium ore on the island, the revolution against him had erupted too soon afterwards for him to advantage the full potential that would have resulted with a successful completion of the mining contract negotiated with a very interested major U.S. industrial conglomerate.

It was Paloma Jola who said of the dead man, "We were childhood friends."

Jack eyed the surrounding jungle, wondering if their returned gunfire had killed the sniper, or at least forced him into retreat. Of course, there was the other possibility that the guy was still there, his M73B1 telescopic rifle sight now aimed in Jack's direction.

"Now, look at him," Paloma continued. "All it took was one second, and his life is gone."

She bent down and rolled the body to get the rifle beneath it as well as get the man's 9-mm largo Spanish Super Star pistol; there were as many countries represented by the munitions present on these few thousand square miles of island soil as there were weapons manufactures in the world. She tossed the handgun to Jack who slipped it between his belt and his belly.

Paloma took two ammunition belts off the body, handing one to Jack and slipping the other over her shoulder to join one already there.

As the group left the body and headed into the foliage, Paloma noticed the almost serene expression on Jack's face, and she was, as usual, amazed by how easily he seemed to accept death—any death. It was almost as if he considered bullets, or exploding metal fragments from some German Democratic Republic

K-2 anti-personnel bounding mine, as no more awe-inspiring than the rain that fell so frequently. Paloma had seen death, now, for all of five years of fighting and doubted she'd ever accept it with the cool passivity with which Jack seemingly managed. So many things about him continued to confuse her, including how he'd proved her so wrong in her having literally laughed in his face, six months previously, when he'd offered physically to join "in her cause". She simply hadn't been able, back then, to imagine this baby-faced man foregoing the luxuries of civilization for the hardship and death of the jungle.

It didn't matter that he was from the Grey Zone and might be expected, on occasion, to make occasional short forays into the wild to ascertain a customer's particular needs as they related to what his boss, Kel Meyers, might have for sale. Jack and Kel had been instrumental in supplying Paloma's men with inexpensive arms for years prior to Jack having volunteered to join them in the field.

Paloma no longer laughed at the idea of Jack as an active mercenary. Not only did he sell weapons, but he knew how to use them. He had killed more than his share of Stefano Peletto's men. He'd shown no regret in doing so, either.

"What are you thinking?" Paloma asked him.

"Me? I was thinking how nice it will be when we can have sex in a nice clean bed."

Actually, he'd been wondering, and not for the first time, about the runners that had arrived two days before. They'd remained for over an hour and talked to no one but Paloma who had, afterwards, sent them packing. Two days later, and still Jack had been unable to learn what news they'd brought. He was beginning to think he might never find out.

"Do you miss your fine clothes and comfortable bed?" Paloma asked.

"When I miss them too much, I shall beg your leave to return to them," he said.

Paloma stopped. Jack took two more steps before he realized she was held up behind him. He turned to try and read her expression. Did she know? Had he somehow slipped up? Had someone found the transmitter? Had word leaked as to why he was really here?

He put his finger on the trigger of his Beretta M51, surveying the jungle to either side in a feigned search for unseen enemy.

"Did you hear something?" he asked.

"No," she said, still curiously eyeing him and wondering how he had managed so quickly to get so close to her that her previous lover had willingly transferred himself to another war zone to make Jack's taking his place more convenient. "Did you?"

"You're the one who stopped," Jack reminded, relaxing his index finger without taking it off the trigger. "I thought something was wrong."

"Why are you here?" she asked.

"I believe you defined this as a reconnaissance mission."

"I don't mean, here, right on this particular spot, at

this particular moment in time. I mean, what are you doing, here, in the jungle, at all? What is someone who could have every form of luxury the outside world has to offer doing in the rain, gunk, and mud with a band of revolutionaries?"

"I thought I told you."

"Why *our* particular cause, though, Jack? Why Paloma Jola's war against the Stefano Peletto dictatorship?"

"Why not?" he said with a shrug.

"It's not really your cause, is it?" she said. "How could you possibly know what this is really all about?"

"Perhaps, I just enjoy the adrenaline rush of confronting death," he said.

"Perhaps, but I think not," she said.

"Are you're sure?"

"While you don't seem to fear it, you certainly don't seem to enjoy it in the way to which you infer. I've seen that kind of man about whom you speak. He would rather kill than have sex. Killing *is* his sex. You're not that way. You look on death as merely something necessary in the scheme of things, not something that, in and of itself, excites you."

"Then, perhaps, I'm here to protect an investment," he offered in alternative. "You and yours have put a sizable amount of money into my boss's coffers, these last few years, and we'd like to see you buying more."

"We would likely buy from Kel Meyers whether or not you were here," she said. "Weapons are necessary to a cause such as ours. Kel would get our gold whether you were here or in some safe-and-sound office in Dubai."

"Must there be a reason for everything, then?" Jack asked.

"Yes," Paloma said, "if only because there *is* reason for everything."

"At some time in every man's life, he must stand up and fight, whether here or elsewhere. Why not let it suffice that I've decided to make my stand here—with you and yours? If I can give you no better explanation than that, then, maybe, it's only because I don't really know the complete answer myself."

Paloma took the two steps necessary to come abreast of him. Together, they started off again.

"Does the not knowing really bother you all that much?" he asked her finally.

"You could leave here tomorrow and have all the things we're fighting for," she said.

"Maybe *my* having them isn't enough," he said with a slight smile. "Maybe, I want *you* to have them, too."

"In five days, we'll be having that sex you want so badly in a clean bed," she said. "It'll be a bonus in being Stefano Peletto's bed."

Jack's mind raced to provide a proper response. He couldn't act too inquisitive; yet, he didn't dare let such an opportunity slip.

"Five days or five years," he said with a shrug, "it'll be worth the wait."

For a seemingly very long while, he thought she wasn't going to say anything more. His heart beat loudly as he contemplated the risk of asking a pointed question?

"Not five *years*," she said. "I said five *days*, and five days is what I meant."

He stopped. She did likewise. They faced each other.

"The runners brought good news?"

"You know of the runners, then." It wasn't a question.

"Everyone knows of them, Paloma. No one, however, seems to know what they came to say."

"In five days, Stefano Peletto will be dead," she said. "In five days, we will occupy the Presidential Palace. We've bought three of his elite bodyguards. He's to be killed in the very bed in which we'll have sex. Possibly, we'll cavort atop sheets still stained with his spilled blood."

"In five days?"

"Does it make you happy that this jungle fighting is almost over and done? Does it make you happy that you'll soon comb all the lice from your hair and take a hot bath again?"

"I'm mostly happy for you," he said. "I'm happy because you're happy for a dream, after five long years, finally to be realized."

Paloma reached out a hand and cupped his chin so that her thumb pushed deeply into one cheek, her fingers into the other.

"Upon you and me now rests the success of this revolution," she said. "I will never betray it. I've put faith in the reasons you've expressed for joining us, whatever they are, and I've decided to judge them real enough to keep you from betraying us. Have I made a mistake?"

"Of course not."

"Because, one leak of this to Peletto, and all is lost that is now so nearly won."

She searched his face for some sign to give her confidence that she had done the right thing in telling him about what was about to happen. She didn't get it. His verbal proclamation, given, wasn't what she'd hoped for. Nonetheless, she'd told him, thereby placing not only her life, the life of her men, but the success of their long-fought cause, in his hands. Why?

Perhaps, it was because she'd come to trust him. Perhaps, it was because she had to be sure she'd bestowed her trust in the right person.

Her fingers relaxed their grip on his face.

"If you betray me in this, I will kill you," she warned him.

"Of course, you will," he said, "but you have my word that I'll never betray you, your comrades, or your cause to Stefano Peletto."

"I trust you," she said. "God help me if I'm wrong, but I do."

"You won't be sorry, "he said. "Just wait and see."

# CHAPTER ONE

Paloma sat behind the large ornamental desk that Christiva's late dictator, Stefano Peletto, had sat behind. She'd had sex that very morning with Jack in the deceased dictator's large four-poster bed. Jack had grunted sounds of passion into the same heavy-draped room that had, but three days previously, heard the rasping and gurgling of Stefano Peletto choking on his own blood. The island despot was dead. Christiva had been liberated. People still danced in the streets. Bells still chimed; people had crowded around Paloma's triumphal procession as it had wound its way through the town toward the Presidential Palace. Over five years of fighting had ended finally in success for the rebels. At least, that was how Paloma had seen it just three days ago. Now, she saw something else; though, what that something else was she hadn't, yet, quite been able to put her finger on. It was still a puzzle with a few missing pieces. Perhaps, Jack's boss, Kel Meyers, was one or more of those missing pieces. Perhaps, he, head of a vast munitions empire, operating exclusively from within the infamous Grey Zone, would provide a much-needed key.

Paloma heard the Learjet. She got up from the desk and walked through large glass doors to stand on the balcony. It was the same balcony on which Stefano Peletto had so often stood, like the omnipotent potentate he was, as the one-hundred fighter-jet planes of the island's air force had soared close over rooftops.

Now, it was Paloma Jola ensconced in the Presidential Palace, instead of Stefano Peletto, only *one* droning private jet seen and heard.

When her forces had marched triumphantly into the capital, Paloma had expected Peletto's Air Force to be part of the spoils. The air fleet, though, was nowhere to be found. The private Learjet, now circling the city for an approach to the airport would, once landed, be the only jet-powered plane on the island, and it belonged to Kel Meyers.

One-hundred planes and their pilots were missing: disappeared. To where? Paloma had asked that question of countless people, none of whom had an answer. The morning of the day of Peletto's assassination, those airplanes had just taken off and disappeared into thin air. The most obvious person possibly to know the answer was Christiva's Minister of Defense. But he was missing, along with the aircraft and pilots. This, in and of itself, wasn't all that strange, considering rats were so often the first to sense disaster and abandon a sinking ship.

The white fuselage of Kel Meyers's plane caught the sunlight, dropped its nose, and coasted the invisible slide to slip behind the camouflage of palm trees surrounding the airport.

What brought Kel Meyers to Christiva? Did he come to offer Paloma more weapons: more guns, ammunition, tanks, and grenades? Perhaps, but that seemed unlikely. Any such deal for additional munitions could easily have been brokered by Jack.

Kel Meyers had taken control of his father's Grey Zone munitions empire upon his father's death and was rumored to have doubled its net worth within a year. He was rumored to be brilliant, ambitious, and shrewd. He had brought people into his organization, like Jack, who were brilliant and young. Kel had said he didn't want his aides withering on the vine before he did.

Paloma came back to the desk, sat down behind it, and remembered when Jack told her Kel was on the way.

What brought Kel Meyers to Christiva? Paloma was assured it likely wasn't anything minor. Jack remained more than competent to carry out Kel's bidding, just as he'd been doing from the get-go. Kel had supplied rebel forces with munitions almost since the beginning, and, yet, Paloma had never seen him in all that time. He had to be concerned with far bigger wars and conflicts than those just ended on this small speck in the Caribbean Sea. He had his fingers in two sizable conflicts ongoing in Asia, three in Africa, and two in the Middle East. Each of those contributed more to his coffers than the happenings on Christiva ever had.

Already, the limousine sent for him was on its way

from the airport to the Presidential Palace. Already, Jack was seated beside the genius who single-handedly controlled a multimillion-dollar Grey Zone munitions organization.

What had Paloma read in Jack's eyes with every mention of Kel? Admiration? Jealousy? Devotion? Affection? ...*Love?*

Although she had always dreaded Jack would betray her to Peletto, her fears had been ill-founded. That coup had come off without a hitch—except for the missing airplanes. What about those missing airplanes, though? What about Kel Meyers suddenly turning up on her doorstep?

Again, she left the desk, this time for the map that almost covered one wall. She surveyed familiar landmasses, mentally computing how much fuel the planes had had in their tanks, how far they could have gone on it. Such computations were futile. The aircraft could be anywhere in South America, anywhere in Central America, or Mexico, anywhere within a good portion of the southern United States. There was no way Paloma was going to come up with a satisfactory answer, just by looking at a map, to explain whatever the sealed instructions that had been delivered to the Commander of the Christiva Air Force from the office of the Christiva Minister of Defense to send one-hundred jet fighters, and their pilots, to be seemingly swallowed into thin air. Their disappearance was no small matter. Paloma had overthrown a regime without use of those planes, but she couldn't hope to hold the island without them.

Had one of Peletto's clever minions seen the writing on the wall and sent the planes somewhere, to be held in reserve, to be called upon at some time in the future to assist in an orchestrated counter-revolution?

The phone rang. Paloma walked the short distance to answer it. A few seconds later, she replaced its receiver. The car bearing Kel Meyers was inside the city limits. Within a few minutes, the munitions baron would be at the Palace.

Paloma decided to greet him in the entrance hall downstairs. It would make their meeting less formal than if she remained in the far more official surrounds of the Presidential offices. After all, Kel was an ally. He had supplied the weapons which had won Paloma her victory. There was the existing rumor he'd somehow— Paloma certainly without a clue—even played some part in the assassination of the dictator. For whatever his assist, weapons and otherwise, fact or fiction, she'd be eternally grateful. Also, he had given her Jack. Or, if not given—what man was free to give another?— he had, at least, been instrumental in bringing them together.

She stopped at the top of the stairs, and turned to face one of the baroque-framed mirrors that lined the hallway. Five years in the jungle had prematurely aged her, making her look forty, not twenty-five. Not an unattractive forty, in that the fighting, which had left so many participants maimed or scarred, had pretty much left her untouched, but a tired forty, to be sure. She was glad the revolution was finally over, in that she'd really never been a die-hard enthusiast. At twenty, when it had all begun, she'd been quite content with her life in a very nice house, attendance in a very nice university, surrounded by very nice friends, many of the latter children of Stephano Peletto's inner circle. She'd been genuinely distraught when she'd been wrenched from all of that, her mother dead on the living-room floor, her father, daughter in hand, clandestinely whisked from civilization to jungle-living. She hadn't volunteered, either, to fill in for him when he'd been killed; she'd been conscripted as the most logical figurehead-replacement necessary to best keep the movement going.

There was the clatter of guardsmen out front of the Presidential Palace as they came to attention. There were muffled voices in indication the automobile had arrived and was disembarking its passengers. Paloma made a final adjustment to her new uniform and went down the stairway.

Kel Meyers wasn't what she expected. For several moments, it didn't even register that he was the man with whom Jack was presently engaged in conversation. He seemed too young. Paloma had heard he was, like she, in his twenties, but where she looked older than her years, he barely looked out of his teens. His tousled straw-blond hair was made more noticeable side-by-side with Jack sable locks. His violet eyes were arched by brows almost brown, set within a startlingly handsome face. His nose was slightly upturned at its tip, his lips full and slightly pouted. There was a dimple in his right cheek that pulsed as he spoke. He wore a stylish, four-button Brioni white-linen suit, with trousers that dropped fashionably close to the floor at the heels of his Gucci boots. He was someone who would look wealthy and well turned-out even among a group of other well-dressed filthy-rich men.

He left off his conversation as did the rest of his group, upon realizing Paloma had come down to greet them.

Paloma could tell, just by the look Kel gave her, that his boyish good looks housed anything but a boy's brain. With his initial once-over, his violet eyes had, indeed, activated a computer-like array of brain cells that began making immediate computations, tallying the results, spewing out conclusions for his future use. With that one initial quick once-over, Paloma felt Kel had somehow perceived more about her than most of her compatriots had done in years of fighting by her side.

He stepped forward, Paloma suddenly realizing Jack had introduced them. Feeling awkward and not really understanding why, she extended her hand, felt the firmness of Kel's fingers as they wrapped hers and squeezed. He was giving her a penetrating stare, but she couldn't bring herself to return it.

"My congratulations on your victory, Madam President," he said.

"We have you to thank for much of it," she graciously replied.

"You're much too kind," he said. He had an enchanting

smile that parted his lips to marvelous advantage over his startlingly white teeth. His grin caused an additional deepening of the dimple in his cheek. A quick movement of his head allowed a few thick locks of his blond hair to feather his forehead and rest their tips in his brows. It was a natural movement—or rather one practiced until it had the appearance of naturalness. In no way did it seem affected and, thus, had a certain charm that most people found exceptionally appealing. It was but one of many such much-rehearsed actions that put people off guard in his presence. Often people found it impossible to attribute brains and/or business sense to anyone seemingly so young and so good-looking. Being suspected not only of youth but immaturity and innocence could give him a decided advantage, in that he was anything but immature or innocent. His brain was far more acute than the majority of his peers.

"Wars are won with weapons," Paloma said. The group moved through the hallway toward the inner courtyard enclosed by the Palace's four main wings. There was shade there, beneath several palms. There were the soothing sounds of water cascading the intricate marble causeways of a central fountain. There were birds, sun, and an atmosphere conducive to bonhomie. It was a beautiful day. The war was won.

"...planes," Kel said to bring Paloma abruptly back from her reverie.

"What?" she was embarrassed she'd lost the first part of the conversation.

"I was commenting upon how, in any war, there will

always be those of us who will make available the guns, bullets, and planes," Jack said. "It takes committed people like you to make them work."

"Those suppliers, other than you, would, I suspect, have provided goods at prices far dearer than you did," Paloma said.

"Such things are always expensive," Kel said and shrugged. "Dealing in as large a volume as I do, however, certainly brings the costs down."

They were in the open, walking the bright sunlight en route to chairs within the shade occupying the opposite side of the courtyard. Paloma was fascinated by the way the light played within Kel's hair. There was hardly any wind, but his lush blond strands moved as if in slow motion, bouncing liquidly, and seemingly possessed of a white-hot glow all their own.

The main players sat down at a table in the shade. Aides, who had accompanied Jack to and from the airport, faded to a discreet distance.

"Would you like something to drink?" Paloma asked.

"Actually, I think I would," Kel said. "Perhaps some local wine?"

"Also, I've taken the liberty of ordering a slight snack," Paloma said. "After your flight, I thought you might be hungry. Nothing too heavy…just fruit and cheese to hold you over until the more substantial meal planned for this evening."

"Sounds like a plan," Kel said.

Paloma motioned the servant awaiting her signal.

"It's quite beautiful here," Kel said. "It's hard to conceive the despot Stefano Peletto assassinated, right here, somewhere within these very premises, just three days ago."

"You knew him, did you?" Paloma asked, following up on the slight suspicion triggered by the tone of his comment.

"We had business dealings, at one time, but always through third parties."

Paloma didn't ask for specifics. Likely, Kel wouldn't have stopped with supplying just her revolutionaries with guns for the just-ended war. He would have found it more financially advantageous to sell to both sides. Now, sitting in the victor's chair, Paloma could afford to be magnanimous, especially since it would have been naïve for her to believe the revolution would have been any easier had Kel not supplied the Peletto regime with weaponry. As Kel had so succinctly put it: whether he sold the guns or not, there were always people who would. The Alfred Krupps of the world had been handing off weapons to both sides long before Kel Meyers, or his father, arrived on the scene.

The servant arrived with fruit, cheese, and chilled white wine. Kel commented upon the delightful "crispness" of the vintage and surprised Paloma by correctly attributing it to a small vineyard in Pavella, a nondescript coastal village, on the other side of the island.

"You'll have to excuse me for bringing up business," Paloma said after sufficient time had elapsed for her to realize that Kel was apparently in no hurry to clarify the reason for his visit. Even as she spoke, she was sure—her thoughts affirmed by his sudden smile—that he'd known, all along, it would eventually come to this moment. "Being new to the chores of governmental administration, still not yet briefed in all the appropriate protocols, I'm still assuming you're here for business and not holiday."

"Jesus, if only it *were* a holiday!" he smiled winningly. He fed a long, firm piece of white cheese into his mouth in a way that would have seemed obscene if not achieved with such artlessness. "Certainly, I could use some vacation time. How I envy Jack his time spent in this tropical paradise."

"It hasn't always been nearly this paradisiacal," Jack reminded.

"I'm joking, of course," Kel conceded. "I've had frequent reports on the progress of the revolution and of the sometimes deplorable conditions within which it was fought."

Paloma wondered from whom he'd received his reports. How many men, in a long succession, might have been Kel's information sources, including Jack York at the head of that list?

She looked to Jack who was directly across the glass-topped table from her. She felt a twinge of jealousy for whatever the bond between Kel and him, but she fought that down. It was silly of her to be envious of whatever the suspected relationship that existed between the two men.

"You're right, though, of course, about this being

business, Madam President," Kel confirmed, picking up one of the white linen napkins and wiping a crumb from the corner of his mouth.

"More guns?" Paloma asked.

"Oh, there will always be the guns I'm prepared to put at your disposal," he said. "Big guns, small guns, anti-tank guns, any kind of guns."

"For a price, of course."

"Of course." He grinned. "This time, though, it's not guns I've come to discuss but planes."

"Planes?"

She waited for him to continue; somehow knowing that, in a few short seconds, missing puzzle pieces might suddenly appear and fall into place.

"I've recently had the opportunity to acquire a number of jet fighters on the open market," he continued. He leaned forward in his chair and reached for another strip of cheese. He swayed the cheese between his fingers before finally biting off its first few fractions of an inch. His even teeth made a clean slice of the whiteness. "Having heard how your own planes seem to have mysterious vanished, I thought, perhaps, we should have this little talk."

"From where did you hear that our Air Force has disappeared?" Paloma asked, surprised when Jack answered.

"I told him."

"I see."

"You surely mustn't hold it against Jack," Kel insisted, finishing off his remaining strip of cheese.

"He was merely thinking of you. Besides, if you must know, your missing Air Force isn't exactly a well-kept secret."

"And what are people saying?"

"That it's one thing to seize power, quite another to retain it. No control of the air puts you at a decided disadvantage. Of course, if your enemies have no planes, either, it could remain stalemate indefinitely. Unfortunately...."

"Peletto's followers have the planes, socked away somewhere in exile?"

"Peletto's followers?" Kel gave Jack a look that expressed either severe disappointment or suspicion the island's new head of state must surely be game-playing.

"Kel is more concerned about several legitimate governments, both in South and Central America," Jack said. "You and I have talked about this before, Paloma."

"It seems to me," Kel said, "that, as of right now, Peletto's followers are the least of your worries. Any attempt they might make will take place at some future date, if just because it'll take them time to regroup, organize, compile finances, and find compatible points for launching any counterrevolutionary moves. But, Madam President, you have several hungry independent nations within flying distance of Christiva that are, right this minute, drooling at the prospects of annexing this little bit of prime real estate. The only thing that's temporarily holding them back is that so many drooling wolves require a particularly brave Alpha Male to risk the displeasure of the others by instigating a seizure. I assure you, though, that this pause is only a short one before the storm. The bait in this case is just a little too tempting not to advantage for very long."

He leaned forward to retrieve his wine glass from the table. He cupped the crystal container between both hands, holding it so that a ray of sun filtered through nearby palm fronds and lit the liquid with a golden flame. He watched the wine for a few seconds before turning his attention back to Paloma.

"Surely, you're well aware of the importance of coro-lundium in providing heat-resistance for rocket cones? Only three deposits of that ore are known in Asia, and those are in communist-controlled countries. Besides the deposit, here, on Christiva, only two other sources in the western world are known to provide quality ore. One of those is in Michigan, USA, and the other is in Cuba. Certainly, the US would like to get its hand on the deposit you have, here, especially since Peletto was on the verge of handing it over to the US when negotiations were interrupted by your little revolution."

"How many planes are you prepared to offer me?" Paloma could see the island already slipping through her fingers.

"I'll give you back your whole Air Force," Kel said.

Paloma was speechless.

"You have the audacity to offer to sell me my own Air Force?"

"I'm a businessman, Madam President," Kel said.

"The island's Minister of Defense, under Peletto, saw the writing on the wall, and it was only natural that he looked out for his own well-being and made provisions by maneuvering the planes off the island and offering them for sale to the highest bidder. There were several potential buyers, of course. You're just lucky the one most favorably disposed toward you and your cause was at the right place and at the right time with the amount of money required to seal the deal."

"Where are the planes, now?"

"Come now, Madam President," Kel said. "We all know that's purely irrelevant at this stage of the game, don't we?"

"You realize that I'll have to check this all out?" Paloma said.

"Of course," Kel said. "Take all the time you need. Or, if not all the time you need, then, at least all the time you feel you can safely afford."

"In the meantime, you'll stay on with us as our honored guest, of course?"

"Of course," Kel said, standing. "Perhaps you would be so kind as to let Jack show me to my room?" Kel bowed stiffly in Paloma's directly. Then, Jack led Kel across the courtyard and through a doorway into the building.

"Do you think this is going to work?" Jack asked Kel, as soon as the men were out of earshot.

"She really has little choice," Kel said. "We haven't lied to her, after all. There might be even less time, though, than we've calculated. You might want to emphasize that to her, at every chance."

"And the planes are where?"

Kel didn't answer.

"You don't trust me?" Jack was disbelieving.

"Of course, I trust you. It's just that I do see how it might be very difficult for you, after all your time spent with the rebels, in the trenches, not to be a little sympathetic, however tentative, to their revolutionary cause. I'm merely reluctant to complicate your life any further."

# CHAPTER TWO

It was late when Jack passed through the sentries on guard outside Paloma's quarters.

"You've been a long time with your friend, "she said.

"We had much to discuss."

"What's he really after?"

"I beg your pardon?"

"Don't either of you take me for a fool, Jack. Up until now, you've at least given me credit for having intelligence. Let's leave me that much now, shall we?"

"Don't you think you'd do better to ask Kel what he's after?" Jack asked.

"I'm asking you."

"He wants you to have your planes. Hasn't he made that clear?"

"He wants more." It wasn't a question.

"He means you no harm," Jack said. "Trust him. Trust me."

"I trusted you once," Paloma said.

"Have I ever gone back on my word?"

"That's a clever way of phrasing it, isn't it?"

"I don't understand."

"Once you told me that you would never betray either me or my comrades…to Stefano Peletto."

"You're surely not saying that I went back on my word," Jack said. "Do you think you would be here, in this room, now, if I'd betrayed either you or your revolution to Peletto?"

"It's not a betrayal *to Peletto* that suddenly worries me. You've managed this all very cleverly. You've come through without ever actually telling me a lie. Yet, what makes me think that you've actually still managed to sell the revolution out from underneath me?"

"Would you like to quit beating around the bush?"

From the very tone of Jack's voice, and his manner, Paloma caught a hint of something previously undetected, by way of insinuation that he was no longer playing second fiddle to her. Through all of their previous relationship, Jack had been but one more of Paloma's men. His position as primary conduit for munitions, and as her lover, had put him a little higher up the hierarchy than most, but he was still just one of the many in Paloma's guerrilla forces. He'd never had any more authority than Paloma deigned give him. During which time, she had underestimated him, in that he had merely done what Kel had wanted him to do and had done it very well, indeed. Now, he wasn't likely to toady up to Paloma, just to please her and keep on her good side. The situation had changed. Kel Meyers had arrived.

"What does Kel want?" Paloma repeated. "I want to

know, now; and, I want to know from you. I want to know exactly. No more play on words. No more being clever. He has what I want, what I need. He knows that, and even knew it before he came here. He has me over a barrel, and you've helped him put me here."

"He isn't another Peletto," Jack said.

"That doesn't answer my question."

"He could have let your enemies have those planes," Jack reminded. "You can check around. You'll find he paid far more for them than anyone actually thought they were worth."

"That doesn't answer my question, either."

"He merely wants a share," Jack said.

"A share of what?"

"I've given you the benefit of intellect," Jack said. "Do you now expect me to spell it all out for you?"

"I want it all out, in black and white."

"You have a country," Jack said. "You have an important mineral deposit. Without Kel, you will soon have neither. The question, then, arises as to whether or not you actually want to keep what you've fought so hard to win. This you can do by merely granting Kel certain concessions."

"What kind of concessions?"

"I really think you should discuss the specifics with him."

"You've acted competently enough as his liaison, so far," Paloma said, "and I see no reason why you shouldn't continue to do so."

"Very well, then," Jack said, "since Kel said it might

come to this."

"How very perceptive of him."

"Don't be bitter, Paloma. Do try to remember than half a pie is more than no pie at all."

"And you'll kindly remember that this island's people compose a nation and not a pie."

"I was speaking figuratively, of course."

"I've decided to make no deals," she said and knew the rashness of her statement before she even finished it. It was painfully apparent that some kind of a deal was going to have to be struck. It was equally apparent to Jack that something was going to have to be worked out. Jack, however, decided to play Paloma's little game, if just for the moment.

"Then, there is no longer any need for further conversation on the subject, is there?" he said.

Paloma turned from the man to the window. There was a moon outside that cast a strange glow over the landscape. Everything seemed bathed in yellow. Paloma felt a sudden chill and turned back to the man who was looking at her.

"Kel has ambitions that have outgrown the Grey Zone," Jack said. "He's known for some time, now, that there have been hush-hush talks, in more than one high government circle, about having his Munitions Empire forcibly dissolved. Certainly, it's become a consistent embarrassment to U.S. officials that guns killing U.S. servicemen, world-wide, have so often been supplied by Kel. So far, everything has been successfully held in check. Money talks, even in America, and Kel is far more generous than most, but he knows he can't maintain the status quo forever, especially since U.S. opposition is growing as more American young men die in wars fought around the globe. Despite their public relations firms, their payoffs, and their under-the-table campaign contributions, politicians know they still need the man on the street to cast the final vote in elections. Kel wants to consolidate and move his operation to safer ground than the Grey Zone before the proverbial shit hits the fan."

"You mean he wants to move it here."

"It won't be a one-way street, I assure you. He isn't the only one to benefit from such a move. Once he achieves nation-status, he's more than willing to input substantial investment as regards the island's economy. He can make Christiva and you powers to be reckoned with."

"And if I don't want to be a power to be reckoned with. If I just want the world to leave me and this island alone?"

"Your chances of being left alone became nil when that deposit of corolundium was discovered here. Did you ever really think you would be free to win your revolution without someone like Kel in the picture? Don't be a fool! If it hadn't been Kel, it would have been someone, decidedly far worse, possibly even worse than Peletto. You're the leader of your people, now, Paloma. For God's sake, start thinking and acting like it."

"I suppose your friend also has his eyes on the corolundium?"

"No matter how much you try, Paloma, you're not going to make that deposit of ore disappear into thin air, like your Air Force did. It's your and this island's cross to bear. You should merely try to think of ways to make it pay maximum dividends for you and yours. Do you want your people to live their lives in squalor while you lounge around in a palace, like Peletto did?"

"This was to be a simple revolution," Paloma said. "Right against wrong. Freedom against oppression."

"I wonder if your father saw that; government and governing never black-or-white simple."

"Kel had this all planned from the very moment he began selling us munitions, didn't he? Maybe, even before?"

"Yes."

"And were the planes always a part of his plan?"

"You'll find out eventually," Jack said. "So, you might as well hear it from me. Yes, the planes were always a part of his plan, the Christiva Minister of Defense in on it from the get-go."

"You told Kel when Peletto would be killed, so the Minister would know when to move the planes."

Paloma wondered what had become of Jack, the man she had known and trusted. How could they have been through so much together without her having seen that he wasn't a simple someone whose wants revolved entirely around fighting for her cause and admiring her as figurehead of that cause? It worried her that she hadn't seen his Mr. Hyde within his Dr. Jeckle. It likely indicated that she was even less committed to the cause than she'd thought possible. Certainly, she'd been made more tired by all the fighting than even she'd realized.

"Kel might have seen the potential, here, at an early date, Paloma, but he wasn't the last. You can thank Kel's exceptional insight, and inexhaustible bank account, that has allowed him, so far, to outmaneuver the competition as well as he has. Had anyone else gotten those planes, you wouldn't, now, be debating whether to compromise but, rather, negotiating your new government's surrender."

"So, I should be thanking you for your betrayal?"

"Quit taking any of this as a personal slight to you, for Christ's sake!" Jack said. "Start thinking about the bigger picture. Christiva is not *just* you, Paloma. It never has been. The sooner you realize that, the sooner you'll come to be the leader your people need and expect you to be."

Paloma hoped he didn't notice the blush in her cheeks. She had always considered him a rather a spoiled little brat, out playing at war. It was hard to have the brat suddenly turn out to be someone who talked about the revolution as if he knew more about it than she did.

"Kel will talk to you tomorrow," Jack said. "He'll want you to place several of his appointees in key positions within your government."

"Impossible!" Paloma protested.

"Necessary, by way of assurance you'll be keeping to your part of any bargain," Jack said. "You will, of course, retain your position as Madam President."

"I'll be a puppet!" she protested. "Do you think I fought in that stinking hell-hole jungle for years just to be dangled on strings manipulated by Kel Meyers?"

"No one will be a puppet." Jack pacified. "It'll be a cooperative effort. Everyone will work together and...."

"Live happily ever after?" Paloma interrupted and laughed nervously by way of punctuation.

"The sooner you realize very few people in the world ever live happily ever after, the better off we'll all be," Jack prophesied.

Paloma got up out her chair, crossed the floor to the door and threw it open. She really didn't know where she was going. It had been a spontaneous action, no thought out rhyme or reason to it. The minute the door was open, she realized the ridiculousness of her situation. Where was she to go from here? Certainly, the two sentries, who eyed her so curiously, didn't have a clue. She turned, returned to her office, and closed the door behind her.

"I will not do it!" she screamed at Jack.

"Of course you will," he said in a quiet reassuring voice which was genuinely muted in comparison to her lead-in. "You are a kind, caring, and considerate leader who wants only the best for your country and the people in it."

"If I were to refuse, where would Kel be?" Paloma asked, leaned back against the closed door. "He needs me. He needs Christiva. He wouldn't blow his chances for such a perfect setup. He'll take less."

"You're wrong, Paloma," Jack disagreed. "Kel will never take less. If you refuse his terms, he'll sell your Air Force to the next highest bidder. The next time you see those planes, they'll be flying over Christiva and dropping bombs."

"Kel would be cutting his own throat."

"He has far more rope and time to play with than you do," Jack said. "He probably has a good year or more to find another Christiva. With the mess of red tape to be plowed through in a bureaucracy like that of the United States, he might even have more time than that. But, what about you, in the interim? We're not talking about years for you, probably not even months. Haven't your agents given you any substantiating clues that you may well be down to only a few days, at most…maybe only a few hours?"

Paloma was trembling. She didn't know if her chill was from a sense of foreboding, from frustration, or from the unnerving realization that she was suddenly at a loss as to where to turn.

She didn't move. She just stood with her hands still clutching the doorknob behind her, her butt and back pressed tightly into the wood.

Jack had spent enough time with her to know how the woman thought of her revolution. People like Paloma had such high ideals, it was hard for them to compromise, but, while wars were often won by people with ideals, countries left in the aftermath were run by people who couldn't let scruples get in their way. Christiva would know wealth like it had never known.

Kel wouldn't stint with money in effort to make it a showplace for his munitions empire in the Caribbean. Now, it was up to Jack to sooth Paloma's bruised ego and make her see that the best way was often not the path originally chosen.

Paloma knew, the revolution a success, there were now things that had to be done, a government that had to be led, and changes that had to be made to jump-start the economy. What did she know of such things? Perhaps, she'd failed to consider all of that previously because she had never really believed the revolution would succeed. How could a handful of men and women survive against the overpowering odds they'd been pitted against?

Well, they had won, with probably more than one assist from Kel and his deep pockets, and Paloma was painfully aware that the business of governing consisted of far more than buying guns and firing them to kill people. She really had no real knowledge of how to proceed. Her university major had been Fine Arts, not Political Science. She couldn't just stand in Peletto's office and proclaim changes—new schools, new industries, new highways—and see them magically happen.

In contrast, Kel had had a plan not just for the war but for what was to come afterward. What he proposed might well be a welcome lifting of the burden from her shoulders…that she hadn't wanted there in the first place. Wasn't there an old saying about opportunity only knocking once?

# CHAPTER THREE

Her reflection was there for a brief moment: her black shock of hair down almost to her brown eyes, her olive-complexioned skin, her pert nose, her swan-like neck, the firm set of her full lips, her ample breasts, and her flat stomach with indented navel.

Paloma doubled her right fist and rammed the reflecting surface. What had been one image became, for an instant, myriad distortion; then, the jigsaw parted, separated, fell away. All dropped and crashed to the marble floor with a force that sent shards skidding to the far walls.

The door behind her swung open, and two guards, summoned by the noise, almost stumbled over each other in their efforts to get into the room. They stopped short at what they saw.

"Get out!" Paloma shouted, already aware that the warmth running along her fingers was blood from her cut hand.

The two guards retreated, pulling the door closed behind them. Paloma reached for her blouse, discarded to the back of a chair the night before, and she carelessly wrapped it around her injured hand. Her blood oozed into the linen, splotching the whiteness with scarlet. She walked to the doors that opened onto the balcony. She swung them open and walked out into the early-morning sunshine. On a table in the bedroom, behind her, a clock struck nine. Paloma heard it and searched the horizon.

Right on cue, the first jets came into view, black specks against the blue sky. Before long, there were more, their noises louder; the Air Force of Christiva again filled the island's air with dull grey fuselages and the loud roars of engines. Christiva's Air Force had returned home.

Paloma unwrapped her hand to be sure her cut was superficial. Silently, she cursed herself for letting her emotions get the better of her. It had been ridiculous of her to smash the mirror. What did it prove? She could have seriously cut herself. What if she'd severed an artery? What if she'd bled to death on the floor? What would that have accomplished? Nothing! A useless sacrifice. Her five years of battle only to end in a fit of pique.

She was calmer now, forcing herself to breathe more slowly. The sound of the planes was directly, overwhelmingly, overhead. In the city, people were celebrating.

The airborne procession ended to become a helix of aircraft, as first one plane and then another dropped toward the airport and the hangar ready for it. Engine sounds were now a muted drone; the merrymaking of the populace, once again, took precedence.

If only there had been more time. But Kel hadn't been lying when he said the jackals were circling their prey. It had taken very little checking by Paloma to verify all of what he said as true. Diplomatic couriers had arrived at the Palace en masse, expressing sympathy, offering help. And even while the ambassadors spoke their joy at Paloma's success in independence, three of their countries secretly prepared to launch invasions. Paloma had to have the Air Force. There had been no other alternative, and she would have been helplessly vulnerable without it.

One of Kel's recently appointed ministers had found all of the documents and correspondence concerning the deposit of corolundium, including the deal Peletto had been trying to make with the large U.S. mining conglomerate. The U.S. ambassador had been one of the first on the phone after the revolution. He had "things of the utmost importance to discuss" with Paloma, in person, concerning Christiva-U.S. relations.

Paloma could likely turn to the U.S. for assistance, against Kel. It would have found some way to give succor if just to protect its chances of accessing the corolundium. But Paloma wasn't willing to do that. She felt more confident dealing directly with Kel who was one man whose decisions were made on the spot. Paloma's mind reeled with thoughts of having to deal with a foreign military, congress, senate, president, and gamut of red-tape producing bureaucrats, none of whom had the power to make any final decision without months of negotiations, checks, double-checks, balances, and secret meetings.

Paloma had only had to place a few of Kel's chosen appointees in key Christiva government positions, including Jack as second-in-command.

"If I don't agree?" Paloma had asked

Kel had only smiled. It was not a smile that bespoke any real warmth or amusement, either. It was but one final statement that Paloma had really little or no choice but to comply.

"You don't seem any too happy," Jack said, joining Paloma on the balcony.

She turned toward him. The last of the jets had disappeared behind the palm trees concealing the runways of the airport. Jack was dressed in his uniform as second-in-command. It was white with gold buttons and gold-braid epaulets His sable hair and tanned flesh looked exceedingly handsome in contrast. Paloma walked past him, back into the bedroom. As she brushed by him, she detected the faint lime-like aroma of his eau de cologne.

"You've hurt your hand?" He gave the impression he didn't have a clue what might be bothering her.

"A slight accident," she diagnosed curtly. "Nothing serious, I assure you."

A plane which had apparently been a straggler from the original group zoomed over the rooftops en route to join the others at the airport.

Paloma went to the doors of the balcony and slammed them shut with such intensity that the glass in one pane threatened to shatter.

"I'm sorry," Jack said simply.

"I don't want your sympathy!" Paloma said. "What I'd prefer is for you and your friends to get out of Christiva and leave me and my people alone."

"I thought you understood," Jack said.

"I understand that I thought you were my friend, and all the time you were using me. No wonder I could never figure out why you had given up so much to fight for my cause. You weren't fighting for it but for Kel and your own agenda."

With the same force that she had closed the doors, Paloma flung them open. This time, one of the panes did shatter, pieces of it clattering loudly to the balcony.

"Listen to those poor idiots, celebrating!" Paloma said. "They're actually dancing in the streets at the news of your promotion. They're happy for you, actually glad. Does it make you smug that you've played your part so well that the people of Christiva actually believe you're one of them? I'm surprised you're not off celebrating with Kel, even now."

"He's sent me to get you."

"Get me?"

"Don't play innocent, Paloma. It's only proper that Madam President be on hand for this morning's festivities, already begun, as you very well know. Some people are no doubt already wondering just where you are. The Air Force is returned, and there's cause for celebration."

"What do you need me for?"

"You're the President of Christiva," Jack said. "I'll

give you ten minutes to get ready. Shall I send someone in to take care of that hand?"

Paloma looked as if she were going to say something but apparently changed her mind.

"I've a car waiting," Jack said. He turned and left the room.

Fifteen minutes later, the limousine, with its escort of military police, was speeding through the streets to the airport. The drive took longer than usual because of the crowds. Once at the airport, the transport was additionally delayed until more police were called in to make way for the car through the jubilant throng. Paloma kept a stern face, refusing to smile or to wave to the adoring multitudes.

"You might try to look a bit more the triumphant revolutionary leader," Jack said, smiling through the window and waving to the crush of people who seemed undaunted by the brute force of the armed men beating them back to enable the car's progression toward the official stands set up along the runway.

"You know what happened to the original Christiva pilots?" Paloma asked.

"You mean that they're all dead?" Jack replied. "Kel told me."

He turned his attention from the window to Paloma.

"Of the one-hundred Air Force pilots who flew out of here, none returned," she said, managing to sound aghast. "Their replacements all in Kel's pay."

"That shouldn't be upsetting," Jack said. "Quite to the contrary, since those who flew out were all under the impression they were on a mission to eliminate you and your revolution once and for all. Could you ever have considered them loyal even had they returned with the planes?"

Of course, he was right. Perhaps, she was angry because she had somehow thought that, upon the return of the planes, and their pilots, she might, somehow, again have the upper hand.

"I killed more than a hundred men in the six months I was an active member of your guerrilla forces," Jack reminded.

"That was different."

"Oh?" He sounded as if he couldn't quite place the difference and doubted she could either.

The car came to a stop, and the doors opened from the outside.

"So glad you could join us, Madam. President," Kel said, his smile deeply dimpling his cheek. He stepped back, letting her step out into the sunlight. She was greeted by a wave of cheers from people who had gathered to witness and celebrate the return of the island's airplanes. Jack got out the other side, and the three mounted the platform and took their seats.

"Nothing serious I hope," Kel said, motioning toward the dried blood on Paloma's hand.

"No," she replied curtly.

During the next hour, Jack was decorated for his services to the new republic. Kel received the Cross of St. John de Perta Villa. Paloma, against her better judgment, gave a short speech assuring the people that the returned Air Force was final assurance the revolution was successfully over.

All three returned to the Presidential Palace in the same car. Kel and Jack were obviously well-pleased. Paloma was sunk into deeper depression. She couldn't help going back over the past few years, trying to fathom what steps Kel had taken to get so completely in control.

"Christiva's President doesn't seem too horribly cheerful," Kel observed.

"She remains dismayed as to fate of the original Air Force pilots," Jack said.

"Oh?" Kel sounded vaguely curious. "I would have expected her to be thankful such a potential nest of vipers is eliminated."

"That's basically what I told her," Jack said.

"She wasn't assuaged?"

"Paloma is very complex," Jack said with a bit of good-natured mockery.

"Indeed," Kel agreed.

"I'd appreciate it if you didn't talk as if I weren't right here," Paloma said.

At the Palace, they exited the car. Jack and Kel disengaged from Paloma for more whispered conversation.

Paloma went to her rooms. Someone had swept up the broken mirror fragments and the pieces of shattered window pane.

Paloma went into the bathroom, stripped down and took a shower. The dried blood on her hand again turned to liquid. The cut again opened. As she wiped herself dry with a thick Turkish towel, she saw its terry-cloth dapple with red. For not the first time, she checked the laceration for any signs of infection but found none. She returned to the living room and, to her surprise, found Julio Esparto waiting there. He'd been her right-hand man and lover before Jack had entered the picture.

He had masculine good looks that included large brown eyes, thick black brows, and dense ebony lashes. Unlike Paloma, who had given up her jungle fatigues for the more elaborate accoutrements of her new position as head of state, Julio wore jungle camouflage.

"Someone said you were smashing mirrors and kicking out glass panes from French doors," Julio said.

"Misconceptions," Paloma lied.

"It's been a long time," he said. Despite his having been supplanted by Jack, Julio originally held no grudges. He hadn't been one to cry over spilt milk. What did disturb him, now, however, was the gnawing realization that Paloma and he had underestimated Kel's man to the detriment of their revolution. Julio wasn't stupid.

When he had initially heard that Jack would join them in the field, he had laughed, made jokes—with several of his peers—as to how the man's zeal would hardly last through the first weeks of the rainy season. Such joking became less adamant, though, after awhile, as even Julio had come to accept Jack as another viable comrade in arms. As a matter of fact, when Paloma began showing a sexual interest in Jack,

Jack actually seeming embarrassed and almost apologetic toward Julio, Julio hadn't tried all that hard to cling to his sinking personal relationships with Paloma. One rain-soaked afternoon, he'd actually gone so far as to tell Jack there was enough fighting with enemy forces without fighting amongst themselves. Shortly, thereafter, he'd arranged to be transferred to another guerrilla contingent. With that rather blasé attitude, he had possibly made the biggest mistake of his life. With easy surrender, deemed, at the time, an exceptionally civilized and sophisticated way to deal with the situation, he had possibly laid the groundwork for what now showed all indications of cracking the very foundations which he had been building during all the years of his fighting in the jungle.

"It has been a long time," Paloma agreed. There had been a time when she had actually felt genuinely close to Julio. Now, she was merely disturbed by how easily she had tossed their relationship aside to accommodate Jack.

There were seconds of uneasy silence. Paloma furtively glanced around the room for her bathrobe, but she'd left it in the bathroom. She took a chair, anyway, propped both of her feet on the seat of the chair opposite, and simultaneously motioned Julio to sit close by.

"We were both fools," Julio said.

"I beg your pardon?" Paloma didn't really want him to elaborate. She had no doubts but that he would just put into words the very fears she was trying to keep buried inside her.

"We should have fought him," Julio said. "I should have killed him."

"Who?"

"Do I really need to say? If so, I will. Jack York. I should have buried a knife in his guts and twisted it there until he died on the blade."

"Don't be idiotic!" Paloma's accompanying laugh was uneasy.

"He fooled us," Julio said. "I should have seen it. I should have known. Instead, I was too busy trying to act debonair: the good guy who had intelligence enough to know that nothing can last forever. You, I can forgive, but I doubt I'll ever forgive myself or him."

There was another period of uneasy silence. Julio got to his feet and walked to the window. The curtains were pulled back. In the distance, dense jungle grew all of the way to the visible edge of a city gone startlingly white in the afternoon sunshine.

Paloma wanted to say something encouraging that would ease the tension, break the overpowering silence. In the end, Julio spoke, his voice so low that Paloma strained to hear it.

"I am going back," he said. "Back out there. Our fighting isn't finished with this peace."

He turned to Paloma. The sun outside put him in silhouette. For an instant, Paloma saw no face, no features, just a dense shadowy blackness before the window.

"To the jungle?" Paloma heard herself asking the superfluous question.

Julio shifted and took himself out of the glare. Paloma was, again, able to distinguish his features. How familiar they were, too. How many nights had she rested with that body close to hers? Julio's face came even more into focus, aged with the war, as Paloma had aged with the war. His expression was of…hurt? Pity? Knowledge as to the futility of it all?

"I came to ask you to come with me," he said. "We fought all those years not for a place but for an idea. Do you think we've achieved that goal, here and now? We almost had it, Paloma. You and I almost had it. It was right there, within our grasp, and it slipped through our fingers: through yours, because you were blinded by an offering of quicker success; through mine, because I couldn't think of doing anything more than trying to be a good sport. Since neither of us was able to see beyond the end of our own nose, we now find our revolution isn't really over. A new phase has merely begun. This time, I fear our chances of winning are even less than they were before."

"I can't go with you," Paloma said.

"Jack betrayed us, Paloma," he said. "He only mouthed his belief in our ideals and our cause, at the same time selling us out to an enemy far more dangerous than Stefano Peletto ever was."

"I can't go with you." Her voice so low that she even doubted she'd said it—thinking, perhaps, she had only, again, thought her words. She shivered, though, at remembrance of how life had been…in the jungle… dangers and death all around.

"You still love him," Julio said. There was no anger in his voice, nothing but the statement of fact that didn't really need voicing. He had seen it, probably from the beginning, and that was likely why he'd surrendered to its inevitability without a fight. Paloma loved Jack. That love colored her reasoning, then and now. Though Jack had sold the revolution out from under them, Paloma would never fully accept it as betrayal because she loved him.

"Yes," she admitted, surprised to hear her actual voicing of something she'd not ever really accepted until now. But, there was more to it than that. Initially, she had been pulled unwillingly into the revolution, as she'd been conscripted into assuming the figure-head position when her father had died. All of her years in the jungle, she had yearned for what she'd had before. Now, that she had some semblance of what she'd thought possibly lost forever, she simply couldn't bring herself to leave it, and return to jungle guerrilla-warfare.

"And you never ever loved me as much, did you?" he asked.

"There are degrees of love," she alibied.

His laugh rang hollow.

"Don't try to salve my bruised ego," he said. "Love is a two-way street. Had I loved you as much as I now like to imagine, I wouldn't have stood by and watched Jack throw his web around you."

He came from the window, dropped to his knees on the floor before her, wrapped his arms around her legs, and placed a warm cheek against her lap.

"How love can so easily make the reality other than it is."

"I can't help myself, you know?" she said, her fingers automatically combing his lush hair.

"I'll forever hate him for making you love him," Julio said. "I'll forever hate myself for standing by to watch it happen. That said…it isn't Jack with whom we must deal in the end. He would be one thing, but Kel Meyers has cleverly manipulated his minions into key positions of power within the new government. It makes me question if we can ever really win against him, but some of us are convinced we must try. Too many lives have been lost already to let them have died in vain. Too many of our friends and comrades have rotted for our ideals, and some of us feel obligated to fight for those ideals until we've won or are left rotting in the attempt."

"Kel is far smarter and cleverer than Peletto," Paloma said. "He's hardly human…more like an unfeeling machine or computer. He has money, power, weapons…more than Peletto ever dreamed of having."

"It's not the winning," Julio said. "Perhaps I, more than anyone, can see that it's no longer that. Now, it merely boils down to my knowing that what I fought for is what I still have to fight for. If I must die for that, even if it's a lost cause, then, I will."

"Oh, Julio, what is to become of you?"

"Likely, I'll perish in the attempt," he admitted. "I know that, as well as I know I'm standing here, now.

Already Kel erects barbed-wire fences that will secure acres of the machines of war in his arsenal, many of which he will turn against me and whomever comes with me. Possibly, mismatched against Kel, I, simply, wasn't born to succeed in this time in history. Maybe in another time, I might have fared better, but my death will be because I continued though I knew the fighting futile. I'll continued only because to die, as I die, if I must die, is the only honorable way I have left. The question remains, though, Paloma, what is to become of *you*? Will you get what you want by staying put? Because, there are rumors that Kel has already set into motion the plans to eliminate, one by one, those leaders who stood shoulder-to-shoulder with you in the revolution. And once he's rid of them, albeit probably keeping you around longest, because you remain such an ideal figurehead of the new government, will a time arrive when he'll see you as the final string that has to be tied? If so, it'll be his decision, not Jack's; Jack likely unable to offer you any protection, if his protection is what you're counting on."

They swung their heads in unison toward sudden and unexpected sounds of uninvited intruders. Not that any door had been knocked down; the door had never been locked.

"What in the hell?" Paloma demanded.

"Julio Esparto," one of the uniformed men, now full into the room, said. "You are hereby arrested for attempts to sabotage the lawful new government of Christiva."

# CHAPTER FOUR

Although Kel had been avoiding her, since she became so insistent in trying to find out what fate had befallen Julio Esparto, it was as if he'd finally planned for them to meet that particular afternoon…maybe, even, he had…with the sun and the flowers and the cascading water of the natural spring all relaying a pseudo sense of peace and well-being. Where, on all other days, he went riding with two or three guards, this day neither was in sight. Paloma followed him, keeping a safe distance, and making sure that he was actually alone. For the first half an hour, she was able to keep concealed within and behind trees and ferns.

Though Jack had listened more attentively to her queries regarding Julio, he couldn't, or wouldn't, give her a satisfactory answer. To hear him tell it, he hadn't even been aware that Julio was in the capital, let alone in the Palace, until after the general had been arrested. Paloma was quite positive, though, that Kel hadn't held back in telling Jack all there was to know about the Julio arrest, including how compromising it had all been for Paloma.

That said…Paloma's relationship with Jack seemed

to have taken a decided turn for the better. Now, that Kel devoted more and more attention to the running of the government, Jack had more time to spare. Of course, there was no denying the possible alternative that Kel was using Jack to keep Madam President carefully watched.

However, this day, Jack was making final arrangements for the construction of a new ammunition dump at Padilla, and Kel had gone riding alone. Paloma had mysteriously been left alone, too, to saddle a horse, and follow after Kel on the path that led through the forest to a grotto at the other end.

The air was sweet with the perfume of flowers. The air was a warm heaviness that weighed not too oppressively but acted, rather, as a pleasant anesthesia to lull the senses into lazy contentment. In the trees, there were singing birds whose brightly colored plumage could occasionally be quick-glimpsed in amongst the limbs and leaves.

Kel reached the meadow first, Paloma reining in to stay hidden while his horse moved through the tall, flower-speckled green toward the forest which resumed on the other side. Kel was dressed all in white except for his black boots. He held a riding crop, which he didn't use. In the sunlight, his hair resembled finely spun gold that moved luxuriously, shifting in thick waves in response to the gait of his mount. Occasionally, a few strands were scattered by a breath of wind and billowed over the man's face to await his hand to brush them away. As Paloma watched, she, once again, found it impossible to fathom how such a vision of seemingly idyllic innocence was possibly something so genuinely sinister.

He swam nude in the grotto pool. Paloma experienced a voyeuristic pleasure in watching him. Green fronds danced in unseen currents. A moss-covered log was half buried in the mud at the bottom. A ray of sunlight filtered through an imperfect canopy of tree limbs. A staircase of wet stones allowed water to run over them and drop as a small waterfall. The basin that caught the water overflowed at its other end, the resulting cascade bubbling musically through a lattice-work of large and small stones. Kel's horse, its reins dragging the ground, grazed lazily on the grass that matted the borders of the pond.

A dog came from the undergrowth, ran the flat rock that jutted into the pool. The animal was small, brown and white. It barked, wagged its tail, and, then, licked the face Kel offered it. The man laughed, floated on his back away from the ledge and into deeper water. He treaded, called out something Paloma was unable to determine but which saw the dog bark twice and jump into the pool.

The scene—man and dog—seemed so idyllic, so indicative of almost perfect innocence that Paloma felt somehow guilty in having accidently stumbled upon something exceedingly private which could be spoiled by her being there. Yet, she couldn't turn away. She kept her gaze, hardly blinking, on the naked man and the dog as they frolicked as if the world were no more than water, sun, and the immediate jungle around them.

How easy it would be for her to take a rifle from her horse, had she thought to bring a weapon, aim it at the man, squeeze the trigger, and watch him bleed crimson into that pool. Julio would have done it. Julio would have had no qualms at all about sapping all that youthful vitality from that perfect male body. Especially since, as Julio had predicted, more of the people who had fought for years in key positions beside Paloma, had been seized and suddenly were as disappeared as Julio. Jack said those "arrested" had "plotted counterrevolution and insurrection". There were rumors of torture and murder, all at orders from the naked man in the pool.

Weren't animals supposed to know a person's real character? Weren't they supposed to know a person's core? Or, were they sometimes fooled like everyone else? Was Kel's façade so perfect that even a dog could look upon it and not suspect the darkness which actually existed within? If that were the case, then Kel's threat was greater than even Julio could have imagined.

Animal and man climbed free of the water. The dog shook his brown and white fur and splattered wetness. Then, he disappeared back into the underbrush from which he'd originally appeared.

The sun had shifted its position. Paloma had lost all sense of time. Great shafts of light now poured through breaches in the tree limbs: spotlights that seemingly set flowers on fire and reflected thousands for rainbows within in the droplets of moisture still clinging tenaciously to Kel's tanned body.

He passed his palms over his chest and belly as a means of stripping them of wetness. Likewise, he pressed water from his thighs and calves. He stretched upward toward the trees: a movement that took on the aspects of almost pagan worship; so it must have been when men still thought gods existed in trees, in water, in the fiery orb that burned the azure sky.

Dog-like, he shook his blond hair, freeing it of some of the water which it still contained. He turned toward Paloma's place of concealment. He smiled. His white teeth were visible behind coral-pink lips. His violet eyes were clearly visible in the light. He spoke Paloma's name.

For an instant, she thought she imagined it, so carried away had she become in her own fanciful daydreams. But, with the smile still on his lips, he spoke her name again. Then, he sat down on a rock and dropped one foot in the water.

"Will you hide in the bushes forever?" he asked. "Actually, I was rather hoping you'd join me, today, in that it's time, I think, we both had a long talk."

Reluctantly, she stepped from the bushes.

"Good," he said, his smile widening. "I felt a little ridiculous talking to what seemed to be just trees and undergrowth." He patted the stone beside him, by way of invitation for her to sit, though she didn't.

"How long have you known I was here?" She was rather taken back that she'd been discovered.

"As far back as the Palace."

"That long?"

"Does that surprise you? After all, I must be particularly observant, at all times, in my business. You might be surprised as to how many people would wish me harm."

He got up from the rock on which he sat and crossed the grass to where she was standing.

"Why such a sad face, Madam President? I've seen few smiles on it, lately, and it should be a time of great joy for you, yes...what with your revolution successfully won, you established within the Presidential Palace, Christiva in the midst of an economic boom?"

"A lot of my old friends and acquaintances seem to be disappearing."

"Previous friends, I suspect," he corrected. "Many of whom, it ends up, like your friend Julio Esparto, so uncertain of their future within the ongoing scheme of things that they decided to take matters in their own hands."

"So many of them to have made it through the war only to become dead after all the fighting?" Lately, Paloma had taken a headcount.

"I'm wondering, Madam President, what part, if any, you see you playing in the future of Christiva, aside, of course, for remaining the President and figurehead of a successful revolution."

"Did Jack ever tell you that I was actually dragged into participation in the revolution, wishing it had never happened, preferring an immediate return to my own home, and to my own friends, many of the latter the children of those within Stefano Peletto's inner circle? I blamed my mother for getting herself killed. I blamed my father for changing our lives from what they'd once been to become a daily chore for mere subsistence, hunted like animals, in the jungle. When my father was killed, did I willingly rush in to fill the breach left by his dying? No. It was other people who decided that my move up the totem pole would be the most advantageous to continuing the cause. Never once was I believed to have the exceptional leadership qualities, or even the tactical and strategic know-how to keep the revolution alive; I was merely my father's child and that was the best rally-round the real shakers and movers could come up with on such short notice. So, happy as hell that the revolution has been favorably concluded, I see my additional participation in the new government of Christiva as temporary at most, and—believe me when I tell you this—look forward to the day when I can just fade out of all the political aftermath, retire into one of the many condos being constructed on the island, these days, and go back to living a life as near as possible to the one I lived before my father dragged me into all of this. My question to you being.... Is that kind of eventual fade-out something you see as a viable option for me in your way of seeing the scheme of things?"

"Certainly," he said, "I see no reason why that wouldn't be acceptable."

# CHAPTER FIVE

"Do you want to talk about it?" Jack asked.

"I'm not too sure I can even put it into words," Paloma said. "It isn't so much that Julio is dead... although that sounds a bit unfeeling on my part... even if we hadn't been close for a very long time. We'd changed. Our good times had become just memories. What was really frightening was the way Kel dispassionately told me."

"Most likely he merely sees it something that needed to be done," Jack said.

Paloma waited for him to continue, finally realizing he'd apparently said all he was going to say.

"Make me understand," she said.

"Understand Kel?" Jack laughed. "No amount of words, though they be strung into a million phrases, sentences, and paragraphs, will likely let you understand Kel, probably because I doubt anyone understands him—even me. And if I don't understand him, by this point, then I doubt anyone ever will."

"You were/are lovers, right?"

He didn't seem surprised by her query but neither denied nor confirmed it.

"I doubt very much that Kel has the capacity to love anyone; not any more at least. Once, he loved his mother who was raped and murdered before his eyes by rebels in a small country you've probably never heard of, in the days before his father had munitions beyond a few rifles stolen from a local Army barracks. He loved his brother who was a low-life killed in an automobile accident in Nice. Once, Kel, possibly, even loved his father, although his dear daddy never really forgave his younger son's superior business sense. And finally, he once did, I suspect, love Manlin Monroe."

There were more moments of silence. Again, Paloma feared he was finished before she wanted him to be.

"Manlin Monroe?" she encouraged him to continue.

"Kel's greatest and likely last love," Jack said finally. "Not because he consciously rejects all others, but, more likely, because his subconscious has, since Manlin, erected all sorts of barriers against letting anyone get close to him, including me."

"You knew Manlin Monroe?"

"Actually, no. Nor, for that matter, has Kel ever mentioned him to me except once, indirectly. He was cleaning this rifle of his, which is a truly beautiful piece of weaponry—a custom-made Swedish VO Vapen, with Damascus octagonal double-barrels, and nutty-root stock, all intricately engraved with battling stags. I couldn't help but comment on just how exquisite it was. 'A gift from a friend,' he said. That was it. I found out only later, from others, that the friend was Manlin who had been but one more of us denizens of the Grey

Zone, brought into the family business by Kel's father; Manlin, I guess, ended up more of a father to Kel than the real one. Real daddy, in the end, sending Manlin off to Africa to end up bloodily murdered in one of those still all-too-frequent wars wherein the blacks are out to kill every white man in sight."

He stared toward the window, the drapes of which were drawn so that nothing could be seen of the outside.

For a moment, Paloma said nothing. "What is there about Kel, do you think, that manages to so thoroughly suck us all in?"

"You really mean...what allowed him to take control of your revolution?"

"Did he tell you that he and I had sex...at the grotto?"

"As a matter of fact, he did. He was interested in hearing my take on why you consented to let it happen."

"And?" She couldn't help but be curious.

"I said you were merely trying to ferret out clues as to what makes him tick."

"He, like you, sees sex appeal and sex as but more ways to manipulate people and to gain some, no matter how tenuous, control over them," she concluded.

"Paloma?" He waited for her gaze to lock with his. When it did, he held it.

"What?"

"I'm truly convinced he didn't like the answer I gave him."

They sat on the bed, each making a conscious effort to avoid physical contact.

Finally, Jack threw back the blankets and got up.

"You're a fool!" he told her.

Her movement to join him was so swift that he didn't even see her coming until he was reeling from her fist to his face. He stumbled back to the bed, and Paloma towered over him.

"Don't ever call me a fool!" she warned. "I might have been one, once, listening to your promises of love, even as you sold me and the revolution down the river, but I'm not that fool any longer."

"You're still the same fool, all right," he begged to differ. His jaw hurt, but he resisted the urge to touch it.

She jumped on the bed, with him, her body connecting with his and pushing him deep into the sheets, blankets, and mattress. She straddled him and pinned his arms along his sides.

"I said, don't call me a fool!" Her body shook from an onrush of adrenalin.

"Don't you see?" he said, surprised he wasn't even putting up a token struggle. It was weird to feel her so physically dominant over him. Ever since Kel had taken control of the country, Paloma had lost stature in Jack's eyes, even though he'd hardly admitted that to himself. Because of that loss of prestige, however, their sex had obviously suffered. Now, she atop him, he felt a recurring spark of how it had been between them… in the jungle…before Kel arrived.

One of Paloma's hands gripped his chin, squeezed, and held the man's gaze affixed to hers. "I've known what you and Kel were up to since he arrived to sell me back my own Air Force," she said. "My mistake was in thinking, at the time, that I still might hold a few trump cards once the planes and pilots were back in my control. But Kel was just a little too clever and killed all the pilots. All of them for Christ's sake!" She crawled off Jack and off the bed. She went to the window, stared at the same drawn drapes which had so recently seemed the center of his undivided attention

He got up from the bed, reached for his robe, and put it on as he attempted to walk passed her to the door. Her right hand clamped hard on his shoulder, stopped him, and turned him toward her.

"I should kill you!" she said. There were beads of perspiration on her upper lip. Her hands moved to his throat, her thumbs pressing the indent at the base of his Adam's apple. "I should push my thumbs into your throat until you fall in a heap at my feet."

"You've no longer the strength or the guts," he said, a mocking smile playing the corners of his lips. "You possibly had both, once, but not any longer."

Her hands dropped free.

He went to the door, opened it, and stepped into the hallway. When he pulled the door closed between them, he headed for Kel's suite.

Kel sat in a chair, himself in a robe, a glass of cognac in a crystal snifter held in his right hand.

"I've been expecting you," he said.

Jack went to the decanter and glasses on a side table. He poured himself a glass and took a swallow. He poured more cognac and walked over to Kel who motioned him into a facing chair.

"She'll have to be killed," Jack said, after a pause.

"She's definitely planning to join them, then?"

"If she's not planning it, yet, she soon will be," Jack said.

"I thought she was really very convincing when she offered an eventual slow fade into obscurity."

"You really need bone up on your Machiavelli. Nothing of great importance is ever achieved, or retained, without bloody winnowing."

"I'm thoroughly familiar with Machiavelli," Kel said. "Did Paloma say anything at all about any plans already underway for her to join the new guerrilla factions in the field?"

"She might, almost, have let something slip," Jack said, "but she's wary of me after what I did when she confided secrets to me in the past. I wouldn't count on her coming out with the latest specifics to me, considering the use I made of her confidence regarding the timing of Stefano Peletto's assassination."

"She loves you, you know?" Kel's glass was empty, and he stood to get himself a refill. He stopped before a glass display case in which was the rifle Manlin Monroe had once given him. He stood there a full minute before continuing to get more cognac and returning to stand behind the chair in which Jack was sitting. The fingers of his free hand ran the upholstery of the chair's back.

"You're not going to interfere with what has yet to be done, are you, Jack?" he asked finally. "And don't tell me the idea has never crossed your mind."

"I don't know why in the hell my loyalty must be questioned by everyone," Jack said, getting to his feet. "Have I ever—ever—done anything other than what my position with you designated I should do so far as you and your best interest?"

"It's human nature to want what's best for one's self, too," Kel countered. "Do you have any idea what's really right for you?"

# CHAPTER SIX

It was madness for her to come, of course, but that hadn't stopped her. Her guards were dead, merely awaiting discovery. His guards opened the doors for her despite the lateness of the hour. They were used to her nocturnal visits—although she hadn't visited Jack's quarters in over two weeks. The doors closed. She stood inside and listened for sounds of him, hearing none. What was at first relief that he hadn't been disturbed by her arrival was replaced by disappointment that he might not even be there.

Her heels clicked on the vein-marbled floor, and she felt tremendous relief when her boots left stone for the muting thickness of rug. His bedroom was dark, though not completely submerged in it. Two windows were evident, someone having either forgotten, or more probably failed, to shut their drapes. Outside, the town provided a series of buildings in black silhouettes. Beyond that, by way of darker darkness was the jungle.

Jack was in his bed, sheet pulled down from his naked chest to the abdominal ridges of his belly. His head rested on the whiteness of a startlingly white pillow, the tan of his flesh readily evident. His sable hair hung his eyes, over his ears, and fanned the pillow case.

What pulled her here? What possessed her to come with the knife in her pocket? She had left the gun. She was no longer supposed to have one. Kel had banned all firearms except for one authorized military contingent within the Palace complex. He'd learned a lesson from the assassination of Stefano Peletto. All of his presently armed retinue had been screened by the massive computer he'd had shipped to Christiva from some previous hiding place within the Grey Zone. More computers were scheduled to fill the entire third floor of the Palace. It was an electronic age, and Kel was out to monopolize whatever the advantages.

Had Paloma tried to reach Kel's quarters, she wouldn't so easily have managed. She would have been searched. Her knife would have been discovered. She would have been locked up. Kel was looking for an excuse to lower the ax. It was no secret Paloma's importance to his success was no longer what it had once been. More and more people were accepting of Kel's assumption of more and more power.

Paloma no longer even bothered to attend state functions. It was always now just Kel at Jack's side in the receiving lines. And while Kel hadn't yet become so bold as to take Paloma's place at the head of the line—surrendering that position to Jack who remained Christiva's official second-in-command—it was no big secret that persons and powers were always at work to improve Kel's position within the hierarchy. More often than not, these days, Jack would mumble apologies that Paloma wasn't feeling well—insinuating alcoholism—and everyone would nod knowingly, take Kel's hand and fall deeper under his spell.

Many were more pleased by Kel than had ever been by Paloma, including the island's aristocracy who had thrived under Peletto and had become fearful Paloma's success might see them stripped of their fortunes and properties, on the island and abroad. So relieved were they that Kel was a man who obviously valued diplomacy as well as war, that they willingly opened their coffers to provide him more backing than had he forced or tortured it out of them.

No denying, though, that prosperity had arrived in Christiva. Ships lined its docks. Dredges enlarged its harbor. Foreign yachts, with strange-sounding names, anchored in its waters, from which stepped foreigners for conferences at the Palace. There were new schools, new hospitals, and new recreational centers. What did it matter that the government outlawed civilians their rights to carry firearms? What did it matter that a few rebel-rousers were daily hauled off to jail? So what that the U.S. Fifth Estate, now, often referred to the island as "Munitions Baron Kel Meyers' Playpen"? For the first time, in a long time, the inhabitants of Christiva felt relatively safe in their beds at night.

Hungarian Countess de la Renzini arrived with her husband, by way of heralding the jet set having found Christiva. They dined with Kel at their newly constructed villa, but one more of the residences and new hotels along once-deserted island's coastline.

Kel threw a party and opened the Palace grounds to an ever more-adoring multitude that feasted on roast pig and drank beer while Kel held court and devoured Russian caviar and French champagne. Christiva's population saw more food in that one evening than most had seen in their lifetimes. That same evening, José Manbalda, one-time hero of the revolution, was taken from his house, with his wife and two sons, all stood against a dungeon wall and shot. José Manbalda had been one of Paloma's generals. Now, the only generals of hers left alive, besides Jack, had fled, either abroad, or to the jungle.

Paloma risked lives by being where she was. So, why was she there, in Jack's bedroom? Why had she come with a knife in her pocket? She put her hand into one pocket and felt the cool metal of a scabbard that, with a mere press of its release catch, would unfold its blade.

On his bed, Jack stirred in his sleep, possibly sensing, even in dream-sleep, that something wasn't quite right. His eyes opened, and he sat up.

"Who's there?"

"Just me," Paloma said. All she needed—not!—was for Jack to raise the alarm.

"Paloma?"

Her fingers fondled the concealed weapon, although it had become painfully obvious that killing Jack hadn't been her motive in coming. She could have already accomplished the deed, had that been what she wanted. Now, awake, he would prove difficult to kill without a struggle.

"What time is it?" He turned on a bed-side lamp and checked the clock that ticked nearby. He didn't wait for her answer. "My God, it's almost three." He looked to Paloma and wiped stray strands of hair from his sleep-filled eyes.

"I came to say good-bye," she said and watched his expression. She hadn't meant to confess; it, just suddenly, had happened. "I'm leaving tonight, and I came to say good-bye."

"Damn it, Paloma," Jack sounded angry, "you and I both know that you're here to force me into making a choice."

"So, why not make it and call your guards?"

"You're so willing to die, are you?"

"Actually, I only recently made the decision that I wanted to live."

"If you ever had any feelings for me, you would have left without sticking around to put me in an impossible position."

"Once, I asked you not to betray me, and you replied with an answer that satisfied me, at the time, but was actually deceptive. I'm here, now, because, despite everything, I still love you."

"Jesus!" His accompanying laugh caught in his throat as a painful croak.

"Kel and I know exactly where we stand, Jack," Paloma said. "It's only you who occupy the middle ground; but, you can no longer have your cake and eat it, too, even though that's exactly what you want to do. I'm here to make you choose. In that, I'm leaving tonight, one way or another, either for the jungles, or to the dungeons, depending upon whether you come with me or not. Do you love me? Have you ever loved me?"

"I can't choose between Kel and you," he said, simply. "He snatched me from the obscurity of the Grey Zone and made something of me."

"Maybe, then, you should call your guards?"

"Damn you, Paloma!"

She wanted to touch him, so she did. What did it matter? She had come too far now. Whether he called the guards, or didn't, it really made little difference. There was much to be lost, either way. If the guards were called, though, it would be more quickly over. If they weren't called, she'd go off into the jungle (with Jack?), and what would befall them there?

"Come with me," she said. She was on the bed, feeling Jack's body against her. "I love you," she whispered into his ear.

She waited for his reply. Surely, this was one of those fairytale moments foretelling a happy-ever-after ending that proved love did, after all, conquer all.

Jack tensed.

"I simply can't go with you," he said.

"Do you really love him, then, more than you love me?"

"I love you; I love him."

"What or who does *he* love?" she wanted to know.

Jack put a flattened palm to each side of her face. He

used his thumbs to trace the outline of her lips.

"You see things so simply," he said. "If only life could be so simple."

"Please, come with me," she said. "You'll be welcomed with opened arms by people, besides me, who still love you and once fought beside you."

"You don't understand," he said. "Not now, probably never. What I wouldn't give to but make you understand."

"Kel offers you more than I do," Paloma divined.

"You're but a few months of my life," Jack said. "Kel is years."

"And you'll call the guards, and they will haul me away, put me in a cell, stand me against a wall, and kill me?"

He didn't answer.

"I don't fear death," she said. "Really, I don't. I love you so much that I doubt it matters what you do. Even when I saw clearly that you had betrayed me and our cause to Kel, my love for you made me rationalize. I can't stop that rationalization, even now. It'll be there as the last spilled blood oozes from my body."

"I do love you," he said.

After which, they made love: slowly, easily, attempting to coax out each and every bit of passion shared between them.

"I told Kel I would willingly fade into obscurity, one day soon," she said in the afterglow, knowing her final decision had to be made and made quickly, before certain options slammed shut; if they hadn't already closed on her. "He said he could be comfortable with that. What do you think, knowing him as well as you do, Jack? Did he tell me the truth, or is it inevitable that no matter what he may or may not think, now, one day he'll see me as just one more loose end that needs to be tied?"

# CHAPTER SEVEN

"I want you to have this," Kel said. He went to the desk, picked up the rifle resting there. He brought it to Jack.

"I can't," Jack said, recognizing the weapon as Kel's gun from the display case.

"Please," Kel said. "It was given me by a very good friend, and I'd like to give it to another."

Jack took the rifle, feeling the coolness of its expensive workmanship that made it as much an exquisite piece of art as a weapon.

Kel went to the table, poured himself a glass of wine, not offering Jack one.

"We have been friends, Jack," Kel said. "That means something to me, since I've always been surrounded by too few people who I might call that."

Jack saw lines of tension at the corners of Kel's mouth, at the corners of his eyes. Someone else might have missed them, but not Jack who knew him way too well."

"And I shall miss you dearly." Kel finished half his glass of wine in one swallow.

"I'm going somewhere?"

"Certainly, after what happened last night, you can't stay here," Kel said.

So, Kel knew. In the end, Jack wasn't surprised.

"I saw it coming," Kel said, "as far back as the airport that day I arrived on the island. I read something in your eyes, then, that even you might not have recognized at the time."

Jack hadn't found his voice. He watched Kel finish off more wine and go back for a refill. When Kel replaced the glass stopper in the decanter, this time, he caused a bell-tone sound of colliding crystal.

"Is Paloma all right?" Jack heard himself asking.

"Better off, for sure, than the four men assigned to guard her last night...all murdered."

Jack's guts turned to ice.

"At the moment, as far as I know, she's just fine," Kel said. "Not dead, because I'm not yet perfect...because you loved her but were a valued friend to me. Even I'm still capable of appreciating the value of friendship. But she will die, only given a temporary reprieve. In the end, she and all those with her in the jungle will lose whatever the extended game they insist upon playing. I give her what little time she has left, and I give you the same, plus the rifle, in indication of how much I do and did value our past friendship. I just can't help wondering why you didn't slip away with her last night. Surely, she asked you to."

"Yes."

"And? Did you both think you could be her spy, here, in the Palace, as you were once my spy in the jungle?"

"No."

"Of course, you didn't" Kel said. "You knew I'd eventually find out the two of you had been genuinely intimate, and I'd never again trust you. But, yet, you remained."

"Though I love you both, I chose you."

"Obviously, I'm not yet past loving," Kel said, "though my capacity for it recedes daily and will, one day, be gone completely. Nor will I mourn its passing. Love is an inconvenience; people, in general, so often disappointing."

"You're not a machine."

"Would that I *were*," Kel said. "There's just way too much pain in loving. I am no masochist that I enjoy the pain. I have already had too much of it, and it has brought me little lasting pleasure. So, thanks to you and Paloma, I'm closer to blocking out love than I've ever been. For years, I've kept that rifle with me, carrying it around like a baby with its teddy bear or security blanket. I'm ready to part with it, finally, along with all its painful memories and attending baggage. The next time we meet, Jack, there will be no more remembering, no more forgiving. There will be no compromises just because you were at one time a friend who once loved me."

# EPILOGUE

The helicopter landed. The wind conjured by rotating blades caused the grass in the clearing to bow before the disembarking passengers.

Kel's blond hair fluttered his tanned face as he moved with three aides to join three people on the sidelines.

"Sir, it is good to see you, again," Manuel Radinco said, giving Kel a smart salute before offering his hand.

"I hope, now that this business is over, we'll be seeing more of you in the capital," Kel said, giving his general's hand a firm squeeze. "I'm presuming, of course, it *is* finally ended."

"It is," General Radinco said with the evident satisfaction and confidence of someone who had long known his job and how to do it. "As you instructed, I called before the bodies were burned."

The rotors of the helicopter ceased spinning, the aircraft dormant as a fossilized prehistoric bird atop its nest. The six people walked toward the lushness of the surrounding forest and, finally, stepped into its surprisingly cool embrace.

"I hear the contract has gone through with the American mining consortium," General Radinco said as they walked.

"Yes," Kel admitted absently. All around was evidence of the recent siege: abandoned guns and ammunitions, bodies and the sickening stench of decaying and burnt flesh.

General Radinco led Kel around the remains of what might once have been a hut but was now only a bombed skeleton of flimsy boards aligned with no specific rhyme or reason, charred by flames now morphed into occasional puffs of smoke and smoldering ash.

They veered onto another pathway, narrow and closely parenthesized by tall trees, thick vines, and claustrophobic underbrush. It became necessary to walk two-by-two; Kel walked beside the general.

"Your wife sends her love," Kel said, physically using one hand to push a vine out of his way. "She's giving a cocktail party in your honor on Friday."

"She loves any excuse to entertain," Manuel said with a smile.

"General Francisco sends his personal congratulations," Kel said. "He and his wife wish you to join them at dinner prior to the award presentations on Saturday. I hope you don't mind, but I took the liberty of accepting for you. Francisco was invaluable in dealing with the Americans as regards the corolundium."

"Of course." Manuel tried to detect something in Kel's voice, or in the man's manner, that might betray the emotions surely boiling inside him. He detected none.

"After a week of state functions, you're liable to wish

you were back here in the jungle," Kel said.

Manuel actually thought he detected a slight grin on Kel's lips.

"Although, I can't imagine anyone preferring any of this," Kel added. "So many people die in jungles."

They stepped into an opening in the undergrowth. There was a cement bunker at a strategic spot on the pathway. The barrel of a gun protruded from one narrow window. The weapon had no one at its sights, or at its trigger. It was but one more skeleton resulting from the night before when the forces of General Manuel Radinco had overrun the area.

"They died in there," Manuel said, pointing to the bunker. "I had the men carry them into the open."

The two bodies in question were laid out, side by side. Five people watched from the immediate vicinity as Kel approached the corpses. Several other soldiers in the more distant periphery stopped what they were doing to watch. They'd heard Kel was coming, but they hadn't actually expected ever to see him in the field.

"How old they both look." Kel's voice was stark in its absence of emotion. He turned from the bodies to Manuel. "You may burn them, now." He wrinkled his nose to indicate the corpses had already begun to deteriorate in the time it had taken him to reach them.

That was that. Manuel had expected more. The scene, as played, was absolutely devoid of emotion. After traveling all those uncomfortable miles, via helicopter to get there, Kel was already returning to the aircraft that would fly him to the Palace.

On the way back to the chopper, Kel talked mainly of festivities about to commence in the capital now that the latest rebellion could officially be declared squashed. He made no specific mention, whatsoever, to either Paloma Jola and or to Jack York.

In the clearing, just before embarking the helicopter, Kel took a few minutes to thank those who had fought so valiantly to bring the particular moment to fruition. After which, a dark-complexioned young soldier came up with a long tube of oilcloth cradled in his left warm, even as he saluted smartly with his right hand. There was no denying hero-worship registered on the young man's face.

"Martínez Holeha," the general identified, "who led the assault party that took the bunker."

"A job exceedingly well-done!" Kel put hands on the young soldier's shoulders, leaned forward and kissed him on first one cheek and then the other. Martínez smelled of gunpowder and death.

"For you," Martínez said, presenting the tubular roll of cloth he'd brought with him.

Kel unwrapped the item, and there were appreciative gasps, from all-around, when the exquisite rifle came into view.

"It was in possession of the man defending the bunker," Martínez said.

"To the victor goes the spoils," Kel said, extending the rifle back to the young man. "You are the soldier. You are the victor. Save this for your children. Tell them that you, and so many others like you, were responsible for making Christiva what it is and what it will be tomorrow."

Martínez dropped to one knee, took Kel's hand and kissed it.

"My children and I will follow you until our deaths," he vowed, his large black eyes misting with emotion. "I promise you that on the soul of my dead mother."

Just before he got into the chopper that would fly him back to the Presidential Palace from which he now controlled not only his munitions empire but a whole island country, Kel turned one last time to General Manuel Radinco.

"There will be a small party for you and your wife at the Palace on Wednesday," he said. "Nothing formal, you understand. Just the two of you and a few very appreciative friends."

# ABOUT THE AUTHOR

WILLIAM MALTESE, the internationally bestselling author of novels, short story collections, and his popular Stud Draqual Mystery Series, has published (under various pseudonyms) close to two hundred books in genres including gay and straight erotica, sci-fi, science-fantasy, mystery, romance, western, adventure, espionage, cooking, wine, and children. With a Business/Advertising degree, Maltese enlisted in the U.S. Army, where he achieved and was honorably discharged at a Sergeant (E-5) rank. Presently, he divides his time between the Pacific Northwest and New York City. You can visit his websites or email him at:

www.williammaltese.com
www.myspace.com/williammaltese
www.facebook.com/williammaltese

email: williammaltese@yahoo.com

www.ingramcontent.com/pod-product-compliance
Lightning Source LLC
Chambersburg PA
CBHW031429250626
47155CB00004B/1673

* 9 781479 401246 *

# INCIDENT AT DUPUNU

## *WELCOME TO THE GREY ZONE...*

...And its nefarious and shadowy landscape that knows no international borders.

...Whose each and every individual has special expertise, but no permanent ties or allegiances to any nationalities, countries, or governments. If you want a landmark statue shattered in New York City, a bridge blown in London, a tower toppled in Paris—but don't want any evidence left around to tie you to the crimes—you'll find people in the GREY ZONE who'll sign on to accomplish any and all of that—for a price!

Denim Grady and Gena Mullen are among those in the GREY ZONE who are involved in, or soon will be involved in, the *INCIDENT AT DUPUNU*...

# Borgo Press Books by WILLIAM MALTESE

*Amen's Boy: A Fictionalized Autobiography* (with Jacob Campbell)
*Anal Cousins: Case Studies in Variant Sexual Practices*
*Back of the Boat Gourmet Cooking* (with Bonnie Clark)
*Blood-Red Resolution: An Adventure Novel*
*Catalytic Quotes (Some Heard Through a Time Warp)*
*Dinner with Cecile and William* (with Cecile Charles)
*Draqualian Silk: A Collector's & Bibliographical Guide to the Books of William Maltese, 1969-2010*
*Emerald-Silk Intrigue: A Romance*
*Even Gourmands Have to Diet* (with Bonnie Clark)
*The Fag Is Not for Burning: A Mystery Novel*
*From This Beloved Hour: A Romance*
*Fyrea's Cauldron: A Romance Novel*
*Gerun, the Heretic: A Science Fiction Novel*
*Get-Real Vegan Desserts* (with Christina-Marie Wright)
*The Gluten-Free Way: My Way* (with Adrienne Z. Milligan)
*The Gomorrha Conjurations: An Adventure Novel*
*The "Happy" Hustler*
*Heart on Fire: A Romance*
*In Search of the Perfect Pinot G!* (with A. B. Gayle)
*Incident at Aberlene: An Espionage Novel* (Spies & Lies #1)
*Incident at Brimzinsky: An Espionage Novel* (Spies & Lies #2)
*Incident at Christiva: An Espionage Novel* (Spies & Lies #3)
*Incident at Dupunu: An Espionage Novel* (Spies & Lies #4)
*Jungle Quest Intrigue: A Romance*
*Love's Emerald Flame: A Romance*
*Love's Golden Spell: A Romance*
*Matador, Mi Amor: A Novel of Romance*
*Moon-Stone Intrigue: A Romance*
*Moonstone Murders: The Movie Script*
*Schism on Antheer-D: Science Fiction* (Gods & Frauds #1)
*Schism on Bnth: Science Fiction* (Gods & Frauds #2)
*Slaves*
*A Slip to Die for: A Stud Draqual Mystery*
*Summer Sweat: An Erotic Anthology*
*SS & M: Being Excerpts from the Nazi Death-Head Files*
*Total Meltdown: An Adventure Novel* (with Raymond Gaynor)
*When Summer Comes*
*William Maltese's Wine Taster Diary: Spokane & Pullman, WA*
*Young Cruisers*

# INCIDENT AT DUPUNU

AN ESPIONAGE NOVEL:
SPIES & LIES, BOOK FOUR

## WILLIAM MALTESE

THE BORGO PRESS
MMXIII

INCIDENT AT DUPUNU

# DEDICATION

To all those as intrigued
by covert operations as I am.

# CONTENTS

# PROLOGUE

Paula Tarner's body was made even more golden by the moonlight that filtered into the cabin through the opened porthole. Her tanned flesh shone with a veneering of sweat coaxed through her pores by a summer's heat which lingered well beyond sundown. Her breasts were domed mounds. Her abdomen was slightly concave.

"God, you're beautiful," Frank Pilusi muttered appreciatively.

Paula knew she was attractive, but she always could appreciate any reassurances. When you used your looks to the advantage she did, and always had, it was nice to know you still possessed what was desired on the market.

Her lips were full and sensuous, now shielding the porcelain whiteness of dentist-perfect teeth. Her face was excellent accompaniment to the curves of her definitely female body. Her blonde hair feathered her forehead.

Frank's eyes continued to roam her nakedness.

He was in good shape despite his hectic pace since he'd become president of the republic of Dupunu. The

muscles of his well-knit frame were stretched with the velvety softness of his ebony flesh. Kinky black hair traversed the cleavage formed by his domed pectorals, and taut lower belly.

"You know what I want, don't you?" Frank asked. His white teeth showed behind lips that weren't as thick as the man's blackness might have implied. His face, in general, reflected more of his great grand-mother's lightness while his body was all African. His eyes were black, his lashes and brows black, his hair black and styled in a short Afro.

Paula took the few steps necessary to bring her into convenient nearness to him by the bed. She ran one of her hands along his chest, downward toward his belly. Frank's navel was a thumbnail-sized knot where her fingers lingered.

He broke the contact to drop onto the bed. She sat beside him, the springs and mattress giving farther beneath her weight.

Beneath them, the ship rocked gently on wind-blown swells. Over the mountain peaks, beyond the horizon, a storm was brewing. The night sky, moonlit, was salted with bright stellar constellations, hazed with cataracts from the fog overhead.

Paula's hand again played over his naked flesh, gliding along the contours of his chest, pausing to lovingly play his nipples to hardness.

He shut his eyes, confident she knew what had to be done. She did. She lowered her face lovingly as an explosion ripped the big yacht apart, turning every-

thing and everyone on it into a hellish ball of flame, metal shards, and flying/frying flesh.

# CHAPTER ONE

"Dead!" Winthrop Sanders repeated for emphasis. In truth, the word needed no emphasis. All three in the room were aware of the far-reaching effects of that particular disaster to which he referred. The new African nation of Dupunu hadn't yet completely recovered from the death of its second president.

Denim Grady lounged in his chair, eyeing Gena Mullen. Simultaneously, he kept his ears tuned in on Winthrop's briefing.

Denim was blond, his hair banged over his forehead and tousled as if he'd been in the wind and hadn't bothered re-combing. His rumpled-hair look gave him a boyishness that belied his thirty years. In fact, his face concealed any indications of his ever having left his twenties behind him. He had the perfect skin inherited from his Dutch ancestors, toasted a delicate shade of brown. His eyes were a startling shade of jade, large and dark behind thick, corn-colored eyelashes and beneath full brows. He was handsome rather than pretty, his square chin with its cleft giving him a definitely masculine look. A dimpling of both cheeks was hardly enough to add any suggestion of cuteness to

his butch good looks. His head sat securely on a thick neck that gave way to a pair of large shoulders. His powerful chest was concealed beneath a cream-colored bush jacket whose top three buttons were opened to reveal a matting of blond chest hair. Relaxed as he was, slouched with his right leg hooked over the arm of his chair, he looked every inch one of those graceful cats of the African veld who escaped the sun by sprawling the limb of some hard-won tree.

Gena, the youngest of the trio, and the one upon whom Denim focused most during the entire briefing, was an attractive five-foot-ten. Her blonde hair and tanned peaches-and-cream complexion provided decided complement to Denim's blond good looks.

"Why us, specifically?" Denim asked in a temporary pause. His question was aimed at Winthrop, but his attention remained on Gena—rather on her abundant cleavage. "With almost every official organization within the country working on this, why pull us in from the Grey Zone? Our entering into the investigation, as far as I can see, isn't going to help matters any. And there are already so many people in the field, official and unofficial, they're tripping over each other in efforts to either get facts or to conceal them."

"As you've correctly surmised, other investigations continue to do nothing but contradict each other," Winthrop said. "They're no closer to finding out what happened on that yacht than they were three months ago."

"What makes anyone think either Gena or I is going

to come up with results more satisfactory?" Denim asked.

"You're the best the Grey Zone has to offer," Winthrop said, "and you both have a previous connection to Dupunu."

"Not to mention we were the names your computer happened to spit out," Denim said, "when Almighty computer was stuffed full of facts and obliged to puke out the potential."

"Somehow, you don't find the possible assassination of this country's leader worth a few minutes of your well-paid time?" Winthrop asked.

He'd been given his job, and he certainly was prepared to follow through. This assignment was Classification-One priority; and, questioning the decisions of his superiors in government was never a smart thing to do.

"If anyone would like my opinion, I agree with Denim," Gena said, adding her first comment to the conversation so far. "There are so many good people, really good people, on this already; I can't see how we can come up with anything new while everyone else draws a blank."

"You two aren't just good," Winthrop said, "you're very good. Probably, you're the best...with a lay of the land...and a valuable outside, independent perspective."

"Flattery will get you nowhere," Denim said drolly. The only thing inviting about this assignment was the money and the prospect of spending some time

with Gena. It had been a long time since the two had worked together, just as long since they'd shared each other's bed and body. Actually, it had been five years ago, in this very same African country, before its independence. James Hamoobisi hadn't been elected first president, let alone his successor blown to smithereens. At the time, there was a white Prime Minister, Salin Porter, everyone expecting an eruption between whites and the blacks. In the end, the whites and the blacks compromised, taking sufficient warning from the examples set by at least two neighboring African nations that probably would never recover from their successful black revolutions.

It hardly seemed possible that Denim had been only twenty-five when he and Gena had humped like rabbits in the Dupunu back country, trying to find James Hamoobisi's rebel encampment to keep him and his from thrusting the country into yet another African hellhole. That would have made Gena only twenty at the time. Funny, but she didn't look much older now. Any indication of any sincere mourning over Hamoobisi's death, diagnosed as "cardiac arrest" three years before, seemed over and done.

Now, Hamoobisi dead, his successor, Frank Pilusi, had followed him into whatever an existing afterlife. That was two Dupunu presidents down in a little over five years. The country was only barely making a better showing of its independence than any other newly emerging African nation; except, it was the people at the top of Dupunu politics who were dying, not the

general population. Now, the country had President Sam Kujucu at its helm, and Denim really knew very little about the man who had supposedly been hand-picked by Frank Pilusi as his vice-president; but, from what he had heard, Denim believed Kujucu firmly in the hands of the white minority.

Denim's thoughts surrendered to the present.

"I tell you what I think," he said. "I think this is going to take a very long time and end up going nowhere. All around, people are screaming bloody murder for a solution to this mess. Yet, just as many other people don't really want it solved, afraid it just might get them too involved if any investigation really started extracting all of the pertinent details. After all, a president doesn't get killed easily, even in Dupunu. He does so only within a web of complex political intrigue. Intrigue in extremely high places, I might add; so high that it offers hindrance to anyone seriously trying to get to the actual bottom of things."

"Listen," Winthrop said, deciding on another approach. He really didn't know why he suddenly found himself on the defensive. He was merely supposed to brief these two and send them on their way. "Might I suggest the two of you just give this a try? Before you know it, you may find all interest having blown over, neither of you the worst for wear but a good deal richer."

"Participate just for show, you mean?" Denim asked. "If so, why in the hell pick us for this little masquerade when so many others from the Grey Zone could do just

as well?"

"Denim, it's imperative the world knows this government is making every effort to get to the bottom of this," Winthrop said. "Unlike our more unstable neighbors, we are trying to put forth some semblance of stability. There's a good possibility, as I'm sure even you'll agree, that our second President was assassinated. In civilized societies, such assassinations cannot be simply overlooked because some prominent people are possibly involved up to their necks. In a nation such as ours, still teetering as it is on racial warfare, there are those on the outside looking in who would like to be reassured that a Negro president, elected by this country's majority, wasn't disposed of by elements acting on behalf of the white minority. We have not come so far that we can't erupt tomorrow into a blood bath of white against black and vice versa."

"I wasn't aware that Frank Pilusi was elected by popular vote," Denim countered. He was nit-picking. Frank Pilusi had been appointed by James Hamoobisi, having assumed the presidency only after Hamoobisi's death of a heart attack. Denim knew what Winthrop was trying to say and had gone over all of it when he'd first been approached for this assignment.

Winthrop sighed. He'd said his little bit and was left with nothing else. If these two weren't on board, another less-able duo would have to be brought in from the Grey Zone. However, still hoping for the best....

"Your case dossiers," he said, taking two manila file folders and handing one to each of them. "If you have

any questions, I shall be available to you on a twenty-four-hour basis." He picked up his own small pile of papers, banged them on the table top to align them, and prepared to leave the room. "Good luck to you both."

"Well," Denim said, his eyes back on Gena after Winthrop left the room, "if I have to be stuck on this farce with anyone, I'm glad it's with you."

"Poor Winthrop," Gena said with a wide grin. "I actually think he thought for a few minutes we were going to tell him to shove his investigation."

"I was closer to doing just that than probably even you'll ever know," Denim said.

Gena somehow doubted that. She was well aware that Winthrop hadn't been exaggerating when he'd said Denim was the best the Grey Zone had to offer. If there was anyone likely to find out who was responsible for Frank Pilusi's death, Denim was that man.

She stretched. Her body was momentarily alive with well-proportioned muscle groups shifting beneath her clothes. For a brief moment, her impressive breasts were thrust into even higher relief.

"So, where've you been, lately?" Denim asked, wondering how he could have forgotten how blue her eyes were. "After you finally pulled out of here, I lost track of you."

"Here, there, a little bit of everywhere," she said, running a hand through her hair to better clear it from her eyes.

"Wherever, the work must have agreed with you," Denim said. "You don't look any different than when

we were traipsing the bush looking for Hamoobisi's encampment."

He had to be careful not to tread too clumsily. While they had easily resumed their relationship, here and now, on a level that seemed amicable, they hadn't parted company, last time, under the most favorable of circumstances. James Hamoobisi had insisted on the break up. While Denim had been vaguely flattered that the Negro leader had considered him competition for Gena's affections, he'd been a little upset when Gena had so readily accepted Hamoobisi's ultimatum for severing Denim and her connection. Of course, Denim had since compounded his own theories behind her ready acceptance.

When it had been decided by whites and blacks alike that a general election was the only way to avoid bloodshed in a country which had been controlled for over two-hundred years by a twenty-percent white minority, it hadn't taken too many smarts to see who it was who would be voted in the top slot by a considerable landslide. James Hamoobisi, having fled to the bush to form his own rebel army in preparation for a fight for independence that he, and others, had originally assumed was inevitable, was, in the end, able to see the advantages of a peaceful solution when one was proposed. He had witnessed revolutions in nearby African nations that had resulted in the mass murder of entire white populations; blacks so eager for independence they'd failed to realize the whites were the only ones with any real knowledge of how to keep

the government and the economy in working order. Certainly, Hamoobisi had recognized the advantages of a peaceful black takeover. Before any successful independence could hope to be truly successful, though, there had to be qualified blacks ready to step into each and every position vacated by a white. Such maneuvering took time and a certain degree of cooperation from the whites. Hamoobisi had, thus, consented to disband his Independence Army and place his name on the election ballot. Many whites, with deep pockets, understandably wanted a watchful eye kept on someone elected by popular vote to head the government. Having access to any person sharing Hamoobisi's bed was an understandable intelligence windfall. It was only logical that most everyone, but Denim, came to view his relationship with Gena as an unwanted complication.

Gena's readiness to comply with Hamoobisi's wishes might have been the only thing which kept Denim alive during that period immediately after Hamoobisi's ascension to power. While the whites who had hired him would have certainly hated to lose one of their own to the vindictive whim of a jealous black man, they would have undoubtedly overlooked his murder of Denim under the circumstances. Dupunu's elite had long been exclusively white, and it had no illusions that there was a very tenuous thread keeping them from the fate of other whites in Africa who had attempted to keep the black majorities at bay. If it had come down to a question of their heads or Denim's, there

was little doubt as to which they would rather have seen roll. Gena's apparent ease in shedding Denim had possibly convinced Hamoobisi that Denim was hardly real competition for Gena's affections. And for a man who had seemed sincerely to prefer a bloodless revolution, Hamoobisi had, likewise, seemed to accept the opportunity to show the whites he was other than just another savage.

This wasn't the first time Denim found himself wondering if Gena had actually loved Hamoobisi. Was that really possible? It seemed unlikely the woman could have gone for so long convincing Hamoobisi she loved him if there hadn't been *some* degree of genuine affection between them. If Hamoobisi ever suspected Gena's faking, he certainly hadn't shown it. She'd been sharing the black man's bed up until the very day he dropped dead.

Bastard! That was literally what Hamoobisi had been. His father had been the overseer on the old Petorsburg ranch. His mother had been a cook in the Litzler kitchen. Neither father nor mother had been of breeder stock. Neither father nor mother had any good looks to pass on to their offspring; and it was, therefore, not surprising that Hamoobisi popped clandestinely from the womb, ugly, and had remained that way through maturity. Denim recalled Hamoobisi's face, trying to put himself in that ugly man's shoes. How must Hamoobisi have felt if actually believing someone like Gena had been physically attracted to him? God, he must have been flattered! You had to look

far and wide to find someone who was more physically perfect that Gena.

"Do you have any idea where we should begin?" Gena asked.

Denim was amazed at how she could step into this room, after five years, and act so easily as if nothing had changed. He was uncomfortably suspect that he had never quite gotten over being discarded for that ugly black man, even if he pretended otherwise. Somehow, it made no real difference as to the reasoning behind Gena's breaking off their relationship. What was important was that Denim had been bested.

"What say we get something to eat before we get started?" he suggested.

She picked the restaurant. They ordered steak.

"What exactly were you doing back in the Dwana Territory before I got here, this time around?" Denim eventually asked after half their meals were consumed.

"Do you have a need to know?" she asked with a wide grin.

"Aside from curiosity, probably not," he admitted.

"That's reason enough for me," she said and laughed. "There were rumors of possible trouble brewing on Dupunu's border with the Union of Gumadi. I was sent in with the team delegated to make sure none of the blacks from the neighboring Gumadi were setting up housekeeping. Dupunu has managed to keep favorable diplomatic relations with Gumadi, as you very well know, and its white government wouldn't take too kindly to this country, with a black president, harboring

dissident runaways."

"Find any?"

"Couple of scattered bands that we rounded up for deportation." She took another bite of her steak. "No indication, though, of the kind of trouble everyone feared."

"Someone thought the runaways might be seriously organizing?"

"There's always that worry, isn't there?" she said. "Everyone, here, is sitting on a potential powder keg, you know. One of these days, all holy hell *is* going to break loose, here, or in Gumadi, or in both countries, and no political experimentation going on here is going to have done any damned good, as blacks start killing blacks, and whites start killing blacks, and the killings overspill tenuous national boundary lines."

"Is that what Hamoobisi expected would happen?" Denim asked.

"He was really out of his element in the Presidential Palace," Gena said. "He was more in his element in the wilderness, organizing and working for one specific goal. He was at a loss in the maze of politics. It was a shame, you know? Rather like watching a wild animal go stir crazy within the confines of a zoo."

Denim was tempted, right then and there, to ask if she'd loved Hamoobisi, but he didn't. Maybe a little later, after he'd had a bit more time to re-establish their previous relationship.

"You think the stress of his inability to adapt is what sent him to his early grave?" he asked.

"He had a few good ideas on what would have to be done to assure his country's survival," Gena said, "but he soon found he could trust hardly anyone. He felt mainly alone, and I suppose that might have sent him to an early grave. On the other hand, he did have a bad heart: and that certainly didn't help any."

They finished eating, and Gena picked up the check over Denim's protests. On the way out of the restaurant, Denim was surprised when she suggested they go back to her hotel room for a couple of after-dinner drinks.

Her hotel wasn't far. They walked there. The heat of the afternoon was partially alleviated by a cool afternoon breeze blowing in off the ocean. The hotel was twenty stories and had a doorman. It was largely segregated, by way of guests, in that there were still few Negroes in the country who could afford the rates.

Denim sat on the couch. Gena brought him a Scotch and joined him after opening the glass doors onto the balcony. The city was laid out below, spreading to the docking area on the harbor.

"So, what's been happening with Denim Grady?" she asked. "From what little I've been able to garner from other than the horse's mouth, I'd say you'd done quite well for yourself since I last saw you."

"Not bad, since work is pretty much all I have," he said, wondering if Gena caught the insinuation that there might, once, have been something more.

"Just don't try to tell me you've remained celibate," she said with a smile.

"Okay?" he asked with a smile of his own.

"Anyone special?"

"You've heard no rumors in that regard?" he asked.

"I never believe everything I hear," she said. "I guess that comes from being in our business where too many people too often try to pass fiction off as fact."

"You've managed to become jaded, have you?" he asked, sipping his drink and rolling the tumbler between the flats of his palms.

"Maybe," she admitted.

He finished his drink and jingled the ice in signal for a refill; she complied, bringing him the bottle and letting him pour his own. He put the bottle on the coffee table, glancing toward her now standing in the opened doorway of the balcony, her back toward the room.

"Any ideas who blew up Pilusi in his yacht?" she asked without turning.

"I don't know; and, in case you haven't guessed, I don't much care. Frank Pilusi was a degenerate, his death possibly one of the best things for this country."

"I don't know why they just don't let it rest, either," she said, turning toward him.

"Oh...we both do so know," he contradicted. "It's what Winthrop raved on about all afternoon. As to how we're all actors on this giant stage, performing for an outside world wherein the powerful love to pass judgment over their weaker neighbors. Undoubtedly, even now, the UN lies in wait, hoping to scream chaos, here in Dupunu, just so it can send in troops. They'd love to be camped on Gumadi's doorstep. They've been

waiting for that particular explosion to occur for at least three generations and would likely give anything to help it along."

"Any ideas how a Pilusi assassination might have been accomplished?"

"A bomb, undoubtedly," he said. "The real question, of course, is how a bomb got on board when everyone who embarked was strip-searched, literally."

"Want to tell me if you think all of this is going to end up on President Kujucu's doorstep?"

"Sounds like the latest President actually has an air-tight alibi…even if he is, somehow, involved," Denim said, knowing he wasn't telling Gena anything she didn't already know. "The way I hear it, he was at a sit-down dinner with all the important people in the country who weren't on the yacht. Every guest at the party certainly can't be involved, I would think. What do you think? You're the one with more history with Dupunu politics than I have."

He was surprised at how those words came out by way of accusation. He'd told himself enough times that there had never been anything so special between Gena and him, so why was he doing his spurned lover bit? He was going to have to snap out of it. He was a professional before all else. Gena was, and had been, all professional, too, only having done, and doing, what she'd been paid to do, and apparently doing it very well.

"President Kujucu is a good man," Gena said.

"A little too friendly toward the whites for some tastes." Denim was commenting upon the possible

contradiction in Gena having believed Hamoobisi good, especially for the blacks, and in her believing Kujucu as good while he was showing all indications of being a white-establishment stooge. Or, had Gena ever believed in Hamoobisi?

"Do you think, perhaps, it's the awareness of Kujucu's friendliness with the white establishment that's causes this sudden push to prove neither he nor it is in any way involved in Pilusi's death?" Gena asked.

"I would say that's a relatively safe assumption for us to make," Denim said. "There are as many blacks as whites on this case. Either faction would love, somehow, to unload blame on the other."

It was growing dark outside. The sky on the horizon tinted strips of clouds with bright orange. The sun was a magnified ball preparing to slip into the sea.

"It's been a long time since we got together for dinner and drinks," he said, deciding he was already tired of Dupunu politics.

"Certainly, a lot of water under the proverbial bridge," she said, coming deeper into the room.

"Not very original, by way of a verbal comeback."

"What else does one say after five years?" she asked with a shrug. "I've changed, you've changed. Why pretend any differently?"

"Are you trying to pretend?"

"Oh, I don't know," she said with a shrug. "Maybe for a quick instant, when I saw you in the briefing room, I remembered old times and wished I could go back to them, but isn't there something about never being able

to go home again?"

"I think you've been beaten to that phrase, too," he said. His glass was empty again, but he didn't make any move to refill it. He was comfortable in the fading light and with the euphoria in aftermath of good drinks, good dinner, and good company. He was remembering how much he had so much once enjoyed her, and he knew that he still did. How many people, black and white, had been in and out of his bed since she and he had last parted? He doubted he could even begin to count, let alone, remember them all.

He put his glass on the coffee table next to the Scotch bottle and went to her in the growing dimness.

"It is truly good to see you again, Gena," he said.

He extended a hand, touching her neck, running his fingers down the line of buttons fastening her blouse.

She didn't say anything, but she didn't do anything to stop what he was doing, either.

# CHAPTER TWO

Glen Guillespie had brown hair, cut short but attractively. It was long enough to hang halfway over his forehead but short enough on the sides to leave his ears naked. His eyes were brown, his nose pugged, his mouth a bit too pouty. Already, his body was in that state of decay arising from too little physical exercise from sitting behind a desk all day long. His belly wasn't as firm as it might have been. His pectorals had puffiness indicative of baby fat at an age when baby fat should have no long existed.

He managed to look genuinely surprised when he opened the door and saw Denim standing there; even though, he'd been expecting him and had been unofficially briefed as to how much he could tell him.

Glen worked for Dupunu National Security (DNS). It had been anticipated that Denim would seek out a synopsis of what had been done by the official DNS investigating team on the scene before him. The DNS, as well as any other governmental agency even vaguely concerned with internal security intelligence, or affairs, had conducted—and were still conducting—queries into the late President's death.

"Come on inside, stranger," Glen invited. "I'll get us a couple of drinks. Scotch, isn't it?"

Denim nodded, and Glen went for the booze.

"I won't flatter myself that you've dropped by for a social visit," Glen said as he brought Denim his drink and sat down in the chair facing him. "I hear you're teamed up, again, with Gena Mullen brought back because of some big favor done the white minority in times past."

"What kind of favor?" Denim was curious.

"Pure speculation, I assure you," Glen said. He hadn't really expected Denim to give any credence to it. The country was riddled with rumors, new ones getting started each day. "I did hear it allowed her to stash a nice little nest egg in some Swiss account."

"So, it's Gena with a Swiss account, now, is it? I remember a couple of years ago, it was I who was supposed to have lifted a sack of diamonds off a dead courier and rushed them into hiding."

"You mean you didn't?" Glen asked. "My God, that's the only reason I've been looking forward to seeing you again."

"If I had a fortune in diamonds hidden away, do you think I'd be back here in this pressure cooker of a country, once again, for the money, and waiting for things to explode?"

"Naturally, you're acquainted with the latest pressure-cooker rumor," Glen commented; it wasn't a question. The rumor had been steadily gaining momentum ever since Sam Kujucu had taken over the presidency.

The blacks weren't any too taken by Kujucu's pro-white stance even if he was one of their own. "I assure you, everything is under complete control. That said... everything else I say this evening is for your ears only, except, of course, for sharing with Miss Mullen."

"Have I ever compromised you?"

"No," Glen admitted. "However, you've never before investigated a Dupunu president's murder, have you?"

"It was murder, then?"

"Certainly, that possibility hasn't been eliminated. Confidentially, the DNS's investigation, as well as all others, as far as I can determine, is a mess. I suspect that's something you've already surmised. Publicly, everyone is making demands for the truth. Privately, many of those same people are wishing the whole thing could quietly be swept underneath the nearest rug. Politics have always been messy, especially in Africa, especially in Dupunu."

"If you're waiting for my 'Amen', you have it."

"You want a summation of what the DNS has found so far? One, it's no closer to getting to the bottom of things than it was at the very onset. Two, no one yet seems to know what was happening on board the yacht at the time it exploded: business or pleasure. Three, Frank Pilusi was possibly having an affair with a young woman called Paula Tarner. Tarner was on board the night of the explosion and is presumed dead with the rest. Four, Sam Kujucu, who has the prime motive, in that he was next in line for the top slot upon Pilusi's death, was hosting a large dinner at the time

of the explosion. Five, the yacht was gone over by bomb crews that very evening; it, also, seems unlikely a bomb so large as to have so completely demolished a ship that size could have been casually carried on board, especially with the stringent security precautions taken in regard to all boarding passengers. Six, for what it's worth, the yacht had been scheduled, once upon a time, as a gift for Lawrence Woodside."

"The Prime Minister of Gumadi."

"One and the same. The yacht was originally built on instructions from James Hamoobisi as a gift for Woodside."

"Rather an expensive gift for a black to have constructed for a white, wouldn't you say?" Denim asked. "And why would Hamoobisi have bothered? Gumadi policies regarding blacks never had Hamoobisi overly friendly toward Woodside."

"It was a gift thought appropriately diplomatic by the powers that be, at the time," Glen said. "Dupunu has always maintained a certain economic dependence upon Gumadi. We still have vital trade ties. Continued good relations were assumed necessary enough by Hamoobisi to be worth the swallowing of a few bitter pills. A severance of *any* trade relations between the two countries would have made maintaining a stable government, here in Dupunu, extremely difficult, and such a severance was possible on the part of Gumadi whose white government wasn't any too pleased, at the time, when a black was suddenly handed the presidential reins right next door, even if whites did still hold

key seats in the Dupunu Assembly."

"The gift never presented."

"Hamoobisi died before it happened. At which time, President Pilusi took a liking to the yacht. You're possibly aware he had rather expensive tastes. He did more entertaining on board, during the months of his presidency, than he ever did at the Presidential Palace."

"I hear he spent a small fortune on his orgies," Denim commented dryly.

"You'll have to ask Gena Mullen," Glen remarked with no apparent sarcasm. "She remained on at the Presidential Palace long after Hamoobisi dropped dead, as you may, or may not, recall. It's hardly a secret she and Pilusi saw more than a little of each other as a result. A good many people were confidentially surprised when she fled the country instead of taking up with Pilusi where she'd left off with Hamoobisi. More than a few merely saw Paula Tarner, picked up by Pilusi on the rebound, as a poor substitute."

"Paula has a story?"

"She was a hostess at the Marina Yacht Club, not above turning a trick or two, even with our present president before he was our present president. Kujucu never was a fool, and, I suspect, it didn't take him long to see he'd found, in Paula, someone who would interest Pilusi after Gena pulled out. Kujucu wouldn't have been the first high official to turn pimp in order to rack up bonus points. He needed all of them he could get, considering Pilusi never thought too much of him, believing he was forced on him, as a vice president, by

a lot of influential whites."

"Was he forced on Pilusi by a lot of influential whites?" Denim asked.

"Anything is possible in politics, buddy," Glen reminded. "Actually, there's a very good possibility that there *was* some pressure put on Pilusi to name Kujucu his vice-president. A number of powerful whites in government didn't see Pilusi as much of an ally. If Pilusi hadn't made some concessions to those high-placed whites, they could have possibly found a way to have forced another general election. Pilusi would have had about as much chance of winning the popular vote as that proverbial snowball had of surviving in hell."

"Why didn't these high-placed whites press for another general election, anyway, instead of making due with Kujucu in a political position with little or no power?"

"With Kujucu as Vice-President, he so obviously pro-white, the white minority at least had a foot in the door. Had they moved to throw the polls open in another general election, there was the good possibility someone like Towan Sasuli would have gotten in. That would have made the blacks ecstatic, but the whites would have shit bricks. Both Pilusi and the white leadership factions had more to gain by the compromise than by throwing open the ballot boxes."

"And so when Pilusi dies, Kujucu slips into the empty slot."

"You see why there's really only pseudo squeals ongoing from the whites to get to the bottom of this? If

Kujucu was involved, then probably so was the white faction. That could be damned sticky. Any definite proof of that kind of involvement could turn everything into chaos."

"But the blacks must certainly be hot to get to the bottom of this if Kujucu or white involvement is even a possibility."

"Oh, they are," Glen agreed. "They'd love to find something. The trouble is that not even they have been able to come up with any proof-positive; and, unless they can, there's not too much they can do, politically or legally. There's been nothing seemingly unconstitutional about either Pilusi or Kujucu's rises to the presidency—especially if Pilusi's death was accidental. Without definite proof of white involvement in Pilusi's death, the blacks' hands are tied—at least for the moment. If they start making complaints too loudly about Kujucu, the whites can smugly point out that the blacks seem suddenly not to like the system they so recently approved, only on the grounds that the current president, a president raised to power via official channels set forth in the black-and-white approved constitution, is sympathetic to the whites. They can point out, also, that the whites hadn't complained at Hamoobisi's election even when he'd been pro-black. Nor had they complained about Pilusi being pro-black, either, when he'd taken over upon Hamoobisi's death. As long as everything has proceeded legally, without proof of foul play, the blacks would be risking the loss of a good deal of world sympathy by turning against the very

system they'd approved. A country like Dupunu is not an island, standing alone. It relies heavily on the world outside. The world outside is basically a white world, no matter how those whites may mouth an equality for all races. Give the outside world another country where the blacks are suddenly running amuck, and a lot of important people are merely going to throw up their hands in disgust and be convinced the blacks haven't the brains to even govern themselves, let alone govern whites. At present, there are some blacks in Dupunu who see the advantages of working within the approved system. Thus far, their logic prevails. However, no one is going to guarantee for how much longer it's going to do so. The majority of the Dupunu blacks, no matter how you look at it, aren't that many generations removed from the trees."

"I find myself wondering what I'm supposed to do if I discover proof of a white plot to install Kujucu in the presidency."

"Do you really...wonder, I mean?" Glen asked as if he doubted Denim's sincerity.

"Would you like to venture your own thoughts on how Frank Pilusi got his?" Denim asked.

"Once, I actually opted for some accidental explosion, possibly something gone wrong in the mechanics of the yacht's boiler. Scientific reports, however, tend to hold out that not even an overheated boiler would cause the kind of damage we're talking. They were literally picking the bodies up in pieces that required a hell of a lot of explosives to get that way."

"Now, you think murder?"

"You know what I think, Denim? I think I really don't know what to think. According to experts, a boiler going up wouldn't cause such an extensive disintegration. But to smuggle aboard the explosives needed for that would have called for the cooperation of a hell of a lot of people. And a hell of a lot of people can't be expected to keep a secret so long. I find it a little hard to believe there could have been a bomb plot without some word of it leaking out, either before, during, or after. No one has come up with anything concrete. And, let's face it…blacks are just as familiar with the ways of getting people to talk as we are."

He decided to shift the conversation and did just that: "I met your Gena Mullen once," he said. "It was at an official reception of some kind, as I remember."

"She's hardly *my* Gena Mullen," Denim said.

"Is it true she was the white-faction's main information source in the Hamoobisi *and* Pilusi presidencies?"

Denim didn't answer.

"That was that, by way of scuttlebutt, around the DNS," Glen continued, even though he was aware that Denim's silence was probably an expression of a desire not to discuss the subject. "It concluded that, though Hamoobisi and Pilusi knew she worked for white faction, neither cared. One, she is a very sexy, white, and blonde. Two, it's always best to know your enemy and keep her close. Three, Hamoobisi and Pilusi turned horny as hell whenever they were around her."

"I hope you don't believe everything you hear,"

Denim said.

"It must have been a tremendous boost to their egos to think a beautiful, blonde, white woman was actually interested in them."

"Do you have any facts that Gena ever expressed any more interest in them than was required by the people who were running her?" Denim asked.

"Rumor was that Hamoobisi was truly convinced she loved him, and vice versa," Glen said. "Do you think that's possible?"

"Anything is possible," Denim said.

"I mean, could someone as ugly as he was have actually been duped into believing someone as good-looking as Gena was interested in him beyond reasons of politics?" Glen wasn't ready to surrender the subject.

"Looks aren't everything." Denim was perturbed to be defending the possibility of a mutual love he personally never truly accepted.

"Why do you suppose the whites pulled her out of the Presidential Palace instead of more thoroughly siccing her on Pilusi? Obviously, he was more than receptive."

"Why do I suddenly get the impression my brain is being picked?" Denim queried.

"Is that what it seems?" Glen was all innocence.

"Did your people tell you to pump me about Gena's work for the white factions under Hamoobisi and Pilusi?"

"No," Glen lied. Information exchanges were, after all, two-way streets. "They're going to be aware, however, that you were here this evening. They're

going to expect some sort of reciprocal information for what they'll have rightly assumed I've given you. And they are curious, have always been curious, about Gena Mullen's role in the total picture."

"I'm afraid you've the wrong source in me to fill you in," Denim said.

"But you were with her when she first met Hamoobisi, were you not?"

"True." That, at least, was common knowledge.

"You were also awfully friendly with her, on your own, at the time."

"More rumors?" Denim asked.

"A little more than rumors, actually."

"Then, I confess. Gena and I were quite friendly at the time she met him. However, he didn't like competition, and Gena dropped me like a hot potato." How bitter that was on Denim's tongue!

"You witnessed the progress of their initial acquaintance. Was it spontaneous, do you think, or totally contrived?"

"Why all of this interest in Gena…now?" Denim asked. "It would seem this is all a bit after the fact. She was out of the Presidential Palace before the explosion that killed Pilusi."

"Actually, someone reported having seen her the day the event occurred."

"Here in the capital?"

"Unsubstantiated, as it turns out; as is the suspicion that if Pilusi *was* assassinated, prominent members of the white minority *were* involved. If, and I empha-

size the *if*, any of it is proved more than *just* rumor, it's imperative, for our nation's continued stability, that such involvements remain concealed. The DNS is unofficially quite pleased with the way things have turned out so far. So pleased that we would be quite willing to plug any loopholes the original conspirators might have left. To plug them, I might add, before less sympathetic factors do what they'd do."

"By less sympathetic, I presume you mean the blacks?"

"The blacks do believe it was foul play," Glen said. "We've word of several meetings held by them behind closed doors to ferret out proof that there has been a conspiracy of the whites subversively to regain previous power. I don't need to remind you that no crime is perfect."

"And you're telling me DNS thinks Gena is somehow involved?"

"There's nothing presently tying her directly to anything conspiratorial," Glen said; Denim was all ears.

"Am I supposed to take up on the word *directly*?"

"After Hamoobisi's death, it was accepted, on all fronts, that Gena would continue her role of white-faction informant by becoming the lover of Hamoobisi's successor, especially since Frank Pilusi was so receptive. Initially, everything proceeded quite as expected. On more than one occasion, Gena took advantage after Hamoobisi's fatal heart attack. Why, then, did the whites pull her out? She leaves the scene suddenly, and

President Pilusi ends up with Paula Tarner by way of poor substitute."

"We've already covered that ground, haven't we?"

"What would you say if I told you that, at the time of Pilusi's death, Paula Tarner and then Vice President Kujucu were suspected of being involved in a plot to assassinate President Pilusi?"

"Tarner and Kujucu?"

"Tarner's suspected part, of course, the more interesting. Do you think she could ever have gotten anywhere near Pilusi, with or without a gun, if Gena had still been around?"

"If Paula Tarner was turning tricks at the Marina Yacht Club," Denim commented, "she couldn't have been a complete dog."

"She was very attractive, with very big boobs, but she wasn't in anyway comparable to Gena. When she began seeing Kujucu, I was assigned to take a closer look and, would you believe, never found any hint of explosives? All indications pointed to it likely to be assassination by gun. Neither Tarner nor Kujucu had any identifiable connections to the kind of explosives needed to disintegrate the presidential yacht. You don't rig a charge that big by reading how on the internet."

"Kujucu might have had access to someone."

"If he'd had any contact with an explosive expert—any contact—it would have been picked up on someone's radar, including mine. The blacks could certainly see beforehand what would happen if Pilusi were ever eliminated after his selection of Kujucu as his vice-

president; Kujucu's leanings toward pro-white were never a big secret."

"Where in the hell does all of this leave us?" Denim asked. He'd heard nothing about a planned shooting, but that didn't mean Glen's facts weren't valid. On the other hand, it seemed apparent the DNS had never had definite proof or Kujucu would have been in jail a long time ago.

"It leaves us with a distinctly rotten smell with no identified source," Glen said. "It leaves us with a president mysteriously dead. It leaves us with a man in the Presidential Palace who is not only a probable pawn of the whites but also a possible conspirator in the murder of his predecessor. It leaves us with a very large black population thoroughly convinced they've been fucked, one more time, but unable to pinpoint, at least at the moment, by whom. As long as they're left in their state of ignorance, the status quo will hopefully be maintained."

"Jesus!" Denim said. "What a fucking mess!"

"Isn't it, though?" Glen agreed.

"I think it might be easier to do nothing and let it all pass," Denim said.

"That's what the blacks probably expect us all to do," Glen said. "But you're not that type, are you, Denim? You pride yourself on doing what you're paid for as well as it can be done. Your superiors know that, and that's why you were brought in. If there are loopholes to be found, you'll find them. And, more importantly, if you can't find them, no one can: white or black."

"Do you think whites are involved?" Denim asked.

"Whoever is, or was, involved, should be commended on a job excellently done. As for whites being involved, who knows? They did rather mysteriously pull Gena out of the Palace, but what did they accomplish by getting Tarner next to Pilusi? Paula was stripped down like everyone else on board that night; not even a bullet in her ass-crack."

"It could, I suppose, all come down to a freak accident of some sort, couldn't it?"

"That's always a possibility," Glen agreed. "All tracks covered, as all indications seem to imply, that will undoubtedly end up the official final explanation."

# CHAPTER THREE

Hamie Gallou was envious. He'd always been partial to blonds, possibly because he'd always wished he'd been born one, with blue eyes, which would have been enough to dispel forever all those horrid rumors of black blood in the Gallou bloodline. The whole idea of a Negro in the Gallou woodpile was totally absurd as far as Hamie was concerned. There were plenty of dark-complexioned people who popped from the wombs of racially pure white stock. Certainly, there was no solid proof he'd ever found that Heidi Gallou, his grandmother, had taken in the child her husband fathered by his partly black mistress, Lucretia Fawasi, when Heidi was unable to have children. Lucretia never had been heard to claim the baby was hers; although, some people were always quick to point out that she *had* been reported confined "with pneumonia" for a very long time to a room of the Gallou mansion. How convenient, too, that she had conveniently died not that long after Heidi had supposedly "given birth".

Hamie certainly didn't look Negroid, having typical European features passed on to him via his father and grandfather. His hair was black but not kinky. His

skin was olive but not black. His lips were full but not thick. His nose was actually thin and aristocratic. His eyes were brown, but what in the hell did that prove? Henri Vaeger, bastion of the white community, and chairman of the country club, had brown eyes, and actually looked more Negroid than some Negroes; yet, his family background was never questioned.

Jarn Gallou, Hamie's father, had once told the boy—during one of Jarn's many drunks—that the fault lie in the size of "the Gallou' penis". Jarn's had been the envy of every white who'd ever seen it. Jarn's father had been hung like a horse, and so was Hamie. Thus, illogical thinking attributed *that* to Negro blood. At the time, Hamie actually believed his father. After all, it was flattering to think other boys avoided him only because they were so envious of a penis Hamie had initially always found embarrassingly big. However, as he grew older and discovered there were actually young men without a trace of Negro blood whose cocks were as big, if not bigger than his, he began to suspect his father of merely making rationalizations for something he didn't understand himself. If Jarn Gallou had been part Negro, his father had never admitted it to him, even going so far as to call any such notion "damned foolishness" the one and only time Jarn had asked him outright about it.

Nonetheless, the mere suspicion of his family being tainted by blackness haunted Hamie, especially as he was ostracized from the better schools and clubs.

What disturbed him, and had disturbed his father

before him, was how Heidi and her husband, while acting at home as if their child and grandchild were white, still, for some inexplicable reasons, failed to insist their offspring be accepted on equal footing with the children of their peers in the general community. Maybe they were too fearful of being turned on themselves. Maybe they knew they could fool themselves into believing their masquerade but would never convince their equals. Maybe they just weren't strong enough to convince an already biased community that their son and grandson were legitimate.

God, how much easier it would have been for Hamie to have been born blond and blue-eyed. Whoever heard of a blond and blue-eyed Negro?

"I don't really see anything, here," the blond, jade-eyed man said. "I understand you do design to order, however?"

"Of course," Hamie said, unable to shake the notion that the man looked familiar. Simultaneously, he chided himself for having that cliché read in too many books and seen in too many movies. Still, if this attractive stud could afford even the suggestion that Hamie might be hired to design a yacht to specifications, it was strange Hamie didn't at least know *of* him. Hamie had long made a habit of following all the Dupunu elite, many of whom had snubbed him.

"Can you show me some photos of ships you've already done?" Denim asked. "I understand you designed and constructed Charles Kinbuti's *Zinbaba*."

"You know Mr. Kinbuti?" Hamie asked. Charles

was one of the Negroes who had managed to benefit from the racial policies adopted within the black-white compromise that had resulted in James Hamoobisi's election as first president. He'd made his fortune by organizing a large number of poor famers into pooling their produce for sale to government facilities. His money had bought him a huge house in an unrestricted district—although unrestricted in name only, Negroes having yet to be given even token entrance into exclusive white enclaves like Thousandpalms.

"Not socially," Denim replied, not meaning to insinuate Charles Kinbuti was, after all, black and could hardly, despite his money, be a member of Denim's peer group. "However, the *Zinbaba* was pointed out to me, not too long ago, by Bernard Stellenbauch. He and I agree the ship has exceptional lines."

So, Stellenbauch thought the *Zinbaba* has exceptional lines? That was interesting, since Stellenbauch's *Gloria II* had been contracted through a British firm and, upon its completion, sailed down the African coast for delivery. Stellenbauch, the local representative for the DeBeers conglomerate, could hardly have given his business to a suspected Negro. This made Hamie suddenly even more suspicious of Denim. It seemed inconceivable that any blond WASP, who traveled in Stellenbauch's circle, would risk dealing with Hamie any more than Stellenbauch had.

"Just what is your line of work, Mr. Grady?" Hamie asked nonchalantly, leading Denim toward the office in back.

"Dutch Oil," Denim replied easily. His cover story would hold up even if Hamie went to the bother of checking. "As you may know, we're here setting up oil refineries at Generos."

This was feasible. The Generos fields had come in under Dutch Oil supervision early last year. There had long been talk about building facilities to refine its bulk oil on-site. Several Dutch Oil liaison executives had been in and out of Dupunu over the past few months firming up negotiations.

"You're new in Dupunu, then?" Hamie commented by way of a question, motioning Denim into a chair beside the desk. Hamie settled into the plush black leather of his own swivel chair which felt good against his body, in that it was expensive and Hamie could afford "expensive". His father had drunk up much of the Gallou money, but the family yacht-building business had boomed under the presidency of Hamoobisi and Pilusi. If his suspected Negroid lineage was a hindrance in the days of total white supremacy, it often proved advantageous during times of political flux.

"New, yes," Denim answered. "However, I have been authorized, by my company, to make certain expenditures. We plan on investing a good deal of capital in Dupunu over the next few years, and our executives, destined to be stationed here, are expecting all the comforts of home. Certainly, feel free to check my company's credit rating."

"I'm quite sure Dutch Oil is okay in that regard," Hamie said. "What does concern me, however, is you

not yet possibly aware of our country's still very much existent…ah…social idiosyncrasies."

"I'm afraid I don't understand."

"You mentioned Charles Kinbuti's *Zinbaba*?"

"That's correct."

"That it was pointed out to you by Mr. Stellenbauch?"

"I'm afraid, I still don't.…"

"You didn't, by chance, happen to mention to Mr. Stellenbauch that your company was planning on purchasing a yacht?"

"As a matter of fact, no," Denim admitted. "Authorization for the purchase hadn't come through at the time."

"Then, even though Mr. Stellenbauch was kind enough to mention my name, he didn't actually refer you to me?"

"You did design the *Zinbaba*?" Denim asked.

"You are, I'm sure, aware of Mr. Stellenbauch's yacht."

"Of course."

"Although he was familiar with my work, he went all of the way to England for both the design and the construction of the *Gloria II*. Does that, perhaps, suggest a little of what I'm getting at?"

"I'm not sure."

"Let's just say that as much as I might appreciate your naïveté in regard to your coming to talk to me about a commission, I'm afraid you'd quickly find taking me on would be a vital…social and business… mistake."

"But the *Zinbaba* is a super ship," Denim insisted.

"It would be false humility on my part to disagree," Hamie said, appreciative of the compliment. He was a good designer and ship-builder, damned good, and it was always good for his ego to hear it verified; especially by someone who would so soon be one of the country's white elite.

Was there a sudden knowledgeable light bulb gone off behind Denim's deep jade eyes?

Hamie didn't recall ever having seen anyone with jade eyes. He'd heard once that some American movie star had them, but he couldn't remember which one; one of those big-busted American women, no doubt.

"Dupunu has been under white domination for over two-hundred years until just quite recently," Hamie said. Of course, he could have hurried ahead, suckered Denim into making a written commitment, but what would have been the point? Denim had powerful local friends, like Stellenbauch. Dutch Oil would certainly have the necessary legal connections to find the loopholes in any agreement, written and signed or not. It just wasn't worth the effort or the resulting hassle. He continued. "Despite the fact that there's a supposed mutually agreed upon integration in effect, the whites aren't going to lose their inbred sense of superiority over night. Therefore if Charles Kinbuti has his yacht designed by Hamie Gallou, then no one belonging to the white side of the same coin should have his yacht designed by Hamie Gallou, no matter how exceptionally fine Hamie Gallou's work may be."

"But that's absurd!" Denim protested. He'd noted there had been no mention or insinuation, by Hamie, about the grandfather who'd poked a Negress in the Gallou family woodpile.

"Maybe," Hamie agreed. "However, it's well to accept the facts of life. Things don't change in a minute. The hope is merely that they do *eventually* change. Sure, I could go ahead and design the yacht you're after; likely even a better one. Personally, I do think, though, that it would be ridiculous for you to begin your stay in Dupunu by alienating most of the people with whom you and your company will be doing business."

"But Dupunu has a *black* president," Denim reminded.

"So, indeed, we do," Hamie agreed, "and I'll be the first to admit that I've grown quite well off because of the blacks raised to positions of power under the provision of our country's new constitution."

"I'm really at a loss as to what to say." Denim looked every part the bewildered young executive suddenly dropped into the deep end of a pool where he floundered.

"You needn't say anything," Hamie said. "You've made no commitments, here. If anybody says anything, all you have to do is say you stopped by for a look-see. That's at least authorized. Your friends will probably think it quite clever of you to have done so. I've seen quite a few of my ideas come back to Dupunu incorporated into yachts officially executed in jolly ol' England."

"You mean people actually steal your ideas?" Denim was righteously indignant.

Hamie laughed. Of course, at one time, he'd been upset by that, but it was satisfying to see the unexpected surprise evidenced by Denim who would soon enough find himself one of that very same group.

"I'm actually quite flattered, I suppose," Hamie said. "I like to pretend that what they've stolen today they might come in to buy in a couple more years. But, maybe, that's a bit too optimistic. Why even your Mr. Stellenbauch...." Hamie hesitated. It wouldn't do him any good to bad-mouth anybody. He'd momentarily been carried away. He didn't want to start sounding bitter. He'd merely, somehow, wanted this obviously sympathetic blond man to see how Hamie *was* being persecuted.

"What about Stellenbauch?" Denim had quickly caught Hamie's mention, again, of the name.

"It was, perhaps, incautious of me to mention him, specifically," Hamie said, still anxious for Denim to know even a powerful deBeer's representative wasn't above stooping to steal ideas. "Let's just say that I've noticed a couple English-made yachts, delivered in Dupunu, over the past couple of years, with structural designs pioneered by me as far back as the *Talenluxe*."

"The *Talenluxe*?" Denim thought it much more convenient to have had Hamie bring up the presidential yacht than himself.

"It was a magnificent ship," Hamie said. "It was the first really big yacht I did, and I sometimes still think

it was my best."

"Was? Past tense?"

Hamie opened the top drawer of his desk and began shuffling through a pile of glossy photos. Finally, he found the one he wanted and handed it across the desk to Denim.

"Beautiful," Denim said with genuine appreciation. Of course, it wasn't the first time he'd seen a photo of the pre-exploded *Talenluxe*. It was a sleek ocean-going pleasure ship with which Frank Pilusi had every right to have fallen in love.

"Indeed!" Hamie agreed with no small amount of pride. "Unfortunately, it *was* the yacht on which President Pilusi was entertaining the night he and everyone on board went up in a giant ball of fire."

"Did the powers that be ever decide it was an assassination?" Denim asked, rising to the opportunity. Things were working out easier than he'd expected. He was glad he'd decided on his particular cover. It put Hamie less on the defensive; his dossier stating a definite paranoia as regarded his possible black background. Confronted by other investigating teams, including one from DNS, Hamie had been decidedly perfunctory in his answers. He'd grown actually border-line vehement when one of the DNS team had made a veiled suggestion that the explosion might have resulted from some defect in the yacht's boiler.

"They've decided nothing!" Hamie said, disgustedly. He felt comfortable talking to Denim. Probably, he was fooling himself, but, he found Denim, likely

quick to adapt to the ways of the people with whom he'd be working and playing, still pleasantly amicable. Hamie was painfully aware he usually had no one to whom he could really talk. The whites never gave him the chance to be chummy, and Hamie avoided making intimate friends with any black who gave indications he or she might be willing to go farther with him than a mere employee-employer relationship. It had been no friendship between James Hamoobisi and him which had gotten him the fat contract for the *Talenluxe*. With a Negro president, it would have been impossible to lay that plum construction job in any white man's lap, especially some white man in England. Dupunu, as an emerging African nation, didn't want to begin by sending its money out of country. It was more ideal to give the contract to a local thought-black boy who could actually do the job and do it well, too few Dupunu blacks having acquired sophisticated skills under long-time white domination.

He'd come up with plans for the luxury yacht to rival those of the billionaire Greek shipping magnates, frankly sickened when all of his hard work, all of that beautifully sculptured metal and steel, had gone up in flame.

"Do you think President Pilusi was murdered?" Denim asked.

"I designed that ship," Hamie said, "and there's no way it disappeared in that blaze of fire unless somebody put an explosive on board. No malfunctioning boiler did the job, nor did any other malfunctioning piece of

installed equipment. You can take that as fact from the ship's designer who supervised the ship's construction from start to finish. Every piece of it was top-notch, brand new, and working just fine when installed. It was checked regularly, after the fact, and checked out as in perfect working order up until the very last."

"So, who'd want to kill your president?" Denim asked. Even he found the question naïve, but Hamie didn't seem to notice.

"There's always someone who wants to see a sitting leader dead," Hamie said. He added with genuine vehemence, "Politics are shitty!"

Denim could agree; so many politicians, including now, having provided him with paychecks.

Apparently, Hamie realized he'd drifted into conversation about which he could get very emotional. He decided he'd said quite enough. After all, what did it matter that the *Talenluxe* was no more? It had given him his desired start in the business. There was already talk of a small Dupunu navy in the offing, and Hamie could be pretty much assured of getting a substantial piece of that pie. Still the *Talenluxe* had been such a beautiful piece of work. When it died, it had been as if a part of Hamie had died with it.

"You said you designed the *Talenluxe* for James Hamoobisi?" Denim said. "Actually, I don't recall him being much of a sailor."

"He wasn't," Hamie replied. "He was planning on giving the ship as a kiss-ass gift to the Prime Minister of the country to our immediate east."

"The Union of Gumadi?"

"More damned politics!" Hamie took back the photo and looked at it for a few long seconds, like a father reminiscing over a now-dead child. "I'll never pretend to understand politics".

It was all pretty much the same information Hamie had given, albeit less easily, to the DNS and other investigating teams. The *Talenluxe* had been an authorized construction by then-President James Hamoobisi, first president of Dupunu. It had been equipped with first-class material. It had been an intended gift for the leader of the Union of Gumadi. Hamie was adamant that nothing but deliberately set explosives could have so thoroughly decimated his masterpiece.

Basically, that left Denim where he'd been before. There was always the possibility Hamie had used less than the best materials, salting away the monetary difference resulting from the purchased third-class and the budgeted first-class. However, that had already been thought of, reports in evidence to verify Hamie hadn't stinted in making the *Talenluxe* prime, the ship's first-class equipment all operational at the time it destructed. As Hamie had stated, backed by experts better able to accurately estimate the force and size of the resulting explosion, nothing short of a deliberate explosive device, and a very large one, could have so completely demolished the ship and its occupants on the night in question. Whoever had put the bomb on board would have had to do so after the bomb crew had finished going over the vessel at 6:30 PM, the

explosion occurring at approximately 10:22 PM.

As an apparent afterthought, Denim asked about Paula Tarner. Hamie, with sudden recall, certainly did remember that woman whose blondness he had admired even more so than the blondness of the man before him.

# CHAPTER FOUR

Denim wanted some information on the security procedures utilized the night of Frank Pilusi's death, and Gena volunteered to supply it, since she knew Bagley Tyles.

Bagley had been only a teenager when Hamoobisi had made him a member of his personal security team.

He had blond hair, blue eyes, and a compact body which had been decidedly muscular and masculine from a very early age. More importantly, he was white, and Hamoobisi found it diplomatically expedient to have at least a couple whites in his personal retinue if just to point out he wasn't overlooking the minority. His other token white male, at the time, had been Klaus Kraken, whose early unhappy background in an orphanage had been responsible for his having few strong ties with his own race.

That Gena, a white female, was under the pay of the white contingent of his government had been known by Hamoobisi from the beginning. However, his baser animal instincts had pulled him to her despite a more practical side of him that whispered he was willingly admitting someone into his inner circle who was poten-

tially dangerous. In the beginning, he told himself he would keep her around just for a while, and then cast her aside. By the time he realized he'd become genuinely fond of her, he was reassured that not all the information he provided her, via pillow talk, was passed by her to her white handlers. He found it easier and easier to confide things to her which he wouldn't even hint to his many ministers, and, certainly, not to Frank Pilusi, then his vice-president, who Hamoobisi considered a mental incompetent. However, despite the many nights Gena and Hamoobisi spent together, despite the secrets Hamoobisi willingly came to confide to her, with perfect trust, in her, he could never successfully persuade himself, as hard as he so often tried, that she actually loved him. That incessant doubt often confused him, especially since she was no longer passing on any of the critical information he gave her. If she didn't love him, why give him loyalty? And if her loyalty was feigned, why hold back anything from the people who'd hired her? Hamoobisi had never been convinced the only reason she didn't betray him was out of a fear that such a major outflow of classified information would quickly have been detected and detrimentally traced back to her.

Eventually, he'd given up trying to figure out Gena, basically content with the status-quo.

Up until the time of Hamoobisi's death, Gena was with him in the Presidential Palace. Frank Pilusi made it known he was actually pleased at the prospect of her fulfilling the same role, during his presidency, as she

had during that of his predecessor. Bagley Tyles's position, however, hadn't been quite so secure. Frank Pilusi had been quick to surround himself with an inner circle composed of men he could implicitly trust. That said... he, like Hamoobisi before him, saw the advantages in having token whites wherever, whenever, possible; since Bagley had never given any outward indication of dislike or opposition to the new president, Pilusi had merely transferred him from the most inner circle into the security contingent that had ended up in charge of screening the passengers and crew who boarded the *Talenluxe* on the night the yacht and its passengers went up in a ball of flame.

"Impossible!" Bagley answered the question Gena had just put to him. "If nothing else, Pilusi was certainly aware he wasn't the most popular leader there was. He had security checking security. Even members of his inner circle were stripped naked before boarding. The only person allowed on board without a thorough going-over was Pilusi, and no way was he responsible for the explosives that caused his death."

"What abut Paula Tarner?" Gena asked.

"Strip searched like all the rest. You've some reason to suspect she was complicit?"

"Strictly off the record, there was possibly some kind of conspiracy, in which she was involved, to kill Pilusi."

"Shoot him, you mean?"

"You know about that?"

"Do you know how many times there were rumors

that you were out to kill Hamoobisi while hopping in and out of his bed?" Bagley asked. "Jealous people just like to talk."

"You think any talk of assassination by gun was just that, then—talk?"

"If she was involved in any viable plot to shoot Pilusi, she certainly was playing it cool. We checked it out, at the time, and found no proof whatsoever to substantiate its existence."

"Checked it out how?"

"Normal procedures," Bagley answered. "She was watched—had always been carefully watched for that matter after Pilusi started taking her to bed. Why all of this interest in a shooting that didn't happen?"

"Maybe the bombing was just an alternative plan of action."

"Well, Paula wasn't carrying any bombs the night she boarded the *Talenluxe* to die with everyone else on board," Bagley said. "Neither she nor anyone else who went through security check that night, could have taken explosives on board."

"What if a couple members of your security team were involved? Any chances they could have turned their backs for a couple of seconds and let explosives pass through?"

"That would have required the cooperation of everyone assigned to security that night," Bagley said. "There were ten of us. Each of us was watching the other nine at all times. There's just no way, Gena; no way at all."

"Could anyone have boarded without going through security?"

"There were more guards on board, and around that ship, when she blew, than there were passengers on board. The only way even vaguely conceivable to board without passing through security would have been by using scuba equipment, and it's doubtful even anyone with a wet suit and invisible cloak could have successfully boarded without detection."

"How about explosives planted on the ship's hull under the waterline?"

"We had men in the water, too, Gena. So many, in fact, you could have probably walked on their backs. The underwater sections of the hull were always checked as part of the bomb-detection routine performed rigorously every time the president was scheduled to come on board. The name of the game was always to trust no one."

"Well, somebody blew the ship and everyone on it out of the water."

"Well, when you find out who that was, and especially the why, I know several very curious people in security who would be more than happy to know the details."

"Confidentially, I'm not any too sure I'm ever going to come up with any real answers," Gena admitted.

"And Denim Grady?"

"It's in his nature to try awfully damned hard, of course," Gena said. "However, the whole damned thing is so convoluted, even as he sees it, especially since

there's always the chance Pilusi was merely collateral damage, considering how many other people were on board."

"I'm glad you're the ones assigned this investigation and not me," Bagley said, and that was an understatement. It hardly made any real difference to him who held the top slot in the Dupunu government. Every president needed security, inner circle and otherwise. The gears of rule had kept right on turning even with Pilusi's death—a new president in place. If President Kujucu were to drop dead tomorrow, someone would quickly replace him; and, Bagley's life would still go on.

Gena walked to the French doors giving access to the veranda. The pool beyond the opened doors was bathed in sunlight. Beyond the pool was a gradual drop of the landscape to the city and the sea below. On the horizon, an ocean liner was leaving a whiff of gray smoke behind it.

"Mind if stay for a swim?" Gena asked. She already knew the answer, but she waited for Bagley's reply before beginning to undress.

Bagley and she recognized their mutual attraction years before; however, neither had been about to endanger his/her position with Hamoobisi at the time.

"I think I'll take the rest of the day off," she said, her blouse stripped free of her bare breasts. She sat on a convenient Ottoman to remove her shoes. "From what I've been led to believe, no one is expecting me to work my ass off on this case anyway."

"Not even Denim Grady?" Bagley asked. He was peeling off his shirt. He hadn't planned any immediate dip in the pool, but—aware of where it might lead—he certainly wasn't going to let the moment pass.

"I don't think even Denim knows how much energy he's prepared to devote to this thing," Gena said, one shoe off, at work on the other. "Though he has the reputation for thoroughness, which was why he was brought in, he's viewed this as a labyrinthine mess from the get-go."

"I've heard talk among some blacks," Bagley ventured, his shoes and socks now off.

"What'd they have to say about the price of tea in China?" Gena encouraged.

"They doubt Denim will be putting out his very best efforts. He's white, after all. As for you...well...you can hardly expect them to count on any real results from a white woman so disenchanted with Pilusi that she fled the country rather than continue sleeping with him."

Gena laughed. Her clothes were dropped around her ankles, and she stepped out of them.

"There's also another bit of gossip you might well find of interest," Bagley admitted.

"Always so much gossip! Always so much interest."

They were stark naked. Gena led the way out onto the veranda and to the edge of the pool.

"No black is pleased with President Kujucu," Bagley said; his eyes squinted attractively in the sunlight.

"They really have very little choice but to grit their

teeth and bear it," Gena said.

She would have preferred to dive immediately into the water but delayed to continue the conversation. While she never based too much on mere heresy, Bagley had always had a way of ferreting grain from chaff.

"Kujucu is, after all, where he is through the legal line of succession established under the auspices of a white *and* black approved constitution," she added.

"There's always rebels, yes?" Bagley ventured.

"You think so?" She was, indeed, anxious to hear his opinions on that particular possibility. Of course, she had her own ideas, and had for a very long time, but it was always wise to consider the opinions of others, especially if they were in positions for observing the internal workings of a country's government.

"I certainly do think so," Bagley admitted. He edged one foot over the side of the pool, testing the lukewarm water with his toes. "We've seen what happened in the Congo and in Rhodesia. That *could* still happen here."

"Neither the Congo nor Rhodesia negotiated for a constitution," Gena reminded.

"This country is eighty-percent black," Bagley said. "Not all of those blacks reason beyond gut feelings. They don't have the schooling to compute the advantages of a constitution over the long run. All they suddenly see is a return to where they were originally, only with whites pulling President Kujucu's strings to make him dance. Now, a few blacks do look upon it as merely a temporary setback, but the majority sees it

as whites merely mouthing cooperation under the new system. Try explaining to a few million ignorant blacks that there wasn't some hanky-panky to get Kujucu into the Presidential Palace. First, Hamoobisi. Then, Pilusi. Then Kujucu. What if it was planned that way from the beginning?"

"Planned?" Gena frowned. The heat of the sun was making her sweat. "Even if one could successfully engineer the explosion of a presidential yacht, only God could have scheduled Hamoobisi's heart attack."

"People have been bought off before to make murder seem death by natural causes," Bagley reminded.

"Wait a minute!" Gena wondered if she were correctly following Bagley's line of reasoning. "You're suggesting Hamoobisi didn't die of a heart attack?"

"I'm not *officially* suggesting anything."

"There was the doctor's report."

"No autopsy, though, if you remember."

"It was no secret he had a heart problem."

"It was never a really serious problem, though, was it?" Bagley reminded. "That fact, however, could have made a drug-induced heart attack seem quite real, couldn't it? Who would have suspected Hamoobisi of being murdered? After all, Pilusi seemed hardly a favored substitute by either blacks or whites at the time. After Hamoobisi's death, the blacks actually assumed the whites would successfully lobby for another general election. Such a move was so definitely expected that any suspicions that Pilusi was behind Hamoobisi's death could easily be shunted off

to one side. With the whites so definitely against him and holding, as they did, key seats in the Assembly, Pilusi couldn't easily be seen as someone so confident as to have killed Hamoobisi with expectations of succeeding him. Certainly, the blacks wouldn't have opposed another general election to toss Pilusi by the wayside. Someone like Towan Sasuli would have been more to their liking in the Presidential Palace."

"Interesting."

On the one hand, Bagley was pleased he might have deduced a possibility before Gena had done so; on the other hand, he somehow failed to believe she hadn't yet considered the possibilities he'd offered up.

"Hamoobisi dies," he said, "and everyone thinks there'll be another general election. In fact, the white minority says nothing, or does nothing, to indicate there won't be. Then, after Hamoobisi's cremation, Frank Pilusi makes his rather startling offer that... if allowed to succeed Hamoobisi as president, he'll choose Sam Kujucu as his vice-president. The whites immediately cease any and all inclinations to throw open the polls, and it's no longer quite so inconceivable that Pilusi might have had a hand in Hamoobisi's death. What kind of autopsy can be performed, though, on Hamoobisi's ashes? The blacks certainly have little legal basis for calling for another general election. Pilusi was, after all, Hamoobisi's official appointee. He was black and hardly a white puppet even if he had selected the whites-friendly Kujucu as his vice-president."

"You're suggesting someone merely went one step farther and got rid of Pilusi, just as Hamoobisi might have been gotten rid of? Who? Kujucu?"

"Kujucu or someone behind him," Bagley said. "Don't tell anyone, but I don't think Kujucu has the brain power to have pulled it off alone."

"If any of this were true," Gena said, "isn't it inconceivable there hasn't been a leak of it, somewhere?"

"Would you like to stop and consider what is to be lost by the white minority if ever a leak did occur?" Bagley asked. "I would say repercussions would be quite dire enough to provide incentive for any white to keep his mouth shut."

"Jesus, Bagley, is there anyone but a fool who embarks on a crime and thinks it's perfect?"

"Look what's to be gained if it succeeded, though," Bagley countered. "Blacks get clamped firmer beneath the white minority's thumb than ever before."

The water in the pool looked even more inviting within the encroaching heat of the continuing afternoon; however, Gena still hesitated entering.

"Do you think Hamoobisi would have, ever, in a million years, let Pilusi get close enough to kill him? I was there, Bagley. Hamoobisi never trusted Pilusi and kept him at a distance."

"Pilusi didn't personally have to do the deed," Bagley reminded, knowing that had to be obvious. "It was only necessary for him to get *someone* near to do it—even you."

"Me?" Gena laughed.

Bagley dropped to the edge of the pool, his legs in the water. Gena came down beside him.

"Are you telling me…if you'd been instructed by the white minority, who everyone knew was paying you, you couldn't, or wouldn't, have done it—especially if they'd offered to pay you enough?"

"At some time, during our conversation this very afternoon, I remember you telling me that all those who went to bed with presidents were kept under careful surveillance—or something to that effect."

Bagley grinned, giving her a look that said more than words. Neither of them could be convincingly naïve enough to believe the security watch on her had, at the time of Hamoobisi's death, been as stringent as it had been when she'd first moved into the Presidential Palace.

"You were securely in Hamoobisi's confidence, by then," Bagley said. "He trusted you, making twenty-four hour surveillance of you extremely difficult."

"He never had us watched in the bedroom?"

"He did for a time," Bagley admitted. "We were all very disappointed when he pulled that plug."

"Do you think I could, or would have, betrayed his trust?"

"He was black, wasn't he," Bagley asked; it wasn't a question.

Gena moved her legs, watching and feeling the liquid move against them.

"Listen, Gena," Bagley said; his voice was low and confidential. "I'm just telling you this so you'll know

what some people are thinking. It's important you know, whether involved in Hamoobisi's assassination or not, that some blacks are going to believe you guilty even without a shred of proof. You have to be careful, what with presidents dropping like flies."

Gena sat in seeming thought for several seconds, watching the whirlpools caused by her paddling legs.

"What if was all true?" she asked finally. "What, if by some strange stretch of the imagination, there was a plot that entailed the murder of two presidents? What if I was part of it, feigned my attraction for Hamoobisi just to get close to him and kill him? What would that have you thinking of me?"

"Hamoobisi and Pilusi were black, weren't they?"

Gena slid off the edge of the pool and into the water. She managed little splash, her submerged head and shoulders quickly coming back to break the surface. She shook her mane of hair to clear it of some water. She swam into a position between Bagley's legs, her hands on the edge of cement between his thighs. "I genuinely appreciate your concern, but there's nothing for you to worry about. It's all been nothing but an exercise in conjecture we've been having here this afternoon. Hamoobisi died of a heart attack. He'd known for months his condition was getting more serious. He used to complain of it in bed, and that was the main reason he pulled those security cameras and mikes: he didn't want news of his illness to get out before he made adequate arrangements for a successor *other than Pilusi*. As it turned out, he merely overestimated

the time he had left."

"Even if that's true, there are people who want, and who will, continue to believe otherwise."

"The blacks in Dupunu must be very careful, Bagley," Gena said. "They want so desperately to be respected by the outside world. Yet, so easily they can prove they're of the same barbarian ilk as the Mau Mau in Kenya, and the baby-killers in Rhodesia, who came before them. Do people out for equality within civilized societies dare risk mutilation of men, women and children, with no provocation, save pure speculation? If they do, they do more than appear to be savages: they are savages."

"Aren't they savages, though?" Bagley asked. "Aren't all of us whites, perhaps, making a grave error in expecting civilized reactions, civilized reasoning, and civilized motivations, from something human only in that it stands on two legs?"

Gena seemed to give an answer some thought.

"If I were any sane white, Bagley," she said finally. "I'd get out of Dupunu, without even bothering to pack. Until then...." She tugged him into the pool.

Recovering from the resulting splash he made in the pool, he shook water from his hair and eyes, and treaded water until oriented.

"We might as well enjoy ourselves in Dupunu while we can," Gena said. She was shoulder-deep, her back against one side of the pool. "How nice if we could only spend endless hours lounging around, here, enjoying good company, good food, and good booze."

"You'd soon be bored out of your gourd," he prophesied.

"Probably," she agreed, "but I still think I would like to give it a try."

The water was bath-water warm, offering little relief from the heat of the afternoon, except in being wet. The sun's reflection danced seductively on the water.

# CHAPTER FIVE

Sam Kujucu looked every inch a politician. He had a background that was uncluttered with even a trace of Caucasian blood. Had he not been noted for his friendliness towards the whites, and his arrogance, in general, he might have become popular among his own kind.

He stood six-feet tall and carried one hundred and eighty pounds, mainly lean, hard muscle. He was a rich chocolate color, satiny and smooth. His chest was sculptured, his stomach washboarded. His nose was broad, his nostrils sensuously flared. His eyes, large and black, were set back beneath heavy brows and thick lashes. His lips were full. His hair, cut short, formed a snug skullcap of tightly twisted black curls. He had startlingly white teeth whenever he smiled.

In terms of Americana, he would have probably been called an "Uncle Sam". In fact, the President's first name, being the same as the Negro in the American novel title, caused several of his countrymen to call him just that. Having read Harriet Beecher Stowe's work, he wasn't amused by his nickname; although, he did go so far as to admit to himself he *was* more partial

to the white way of running things than he was to the way of his native brothers. His disenchantment from his fellow Negroes arose partly from his favorable treatment by one particular white man, Chad Pallidin.

Sam Kujucu had been born to Mary and William Kujucu on the Pallidin farm on the outskirts of the Dupunu capital. The Pallidins descended from the earliest white settlers in the country who had arrived long before Sam Kujucu was born. By the time of Sam's birth, Chad had come to consider the blacks on his farm as part of his extended family—albeit the poorer relations. They could almost all be traced back to the first slaves Sean Pallidin had selected from conquered indigenous tribes more than two-hundred years before.

Sean Pallidin, the founder of the "Pallidin clan in Dupunu", was unlike many of his peers in that he early acknowledged his success in farming was dependent upon the cooperation of cheap Negro labor. Intuitively, he knew the best way to get the most work out of animals was not to treat them badly but as if they were almost human. Therefore, he made it his policy, and that of his family, and that of any whites who worked for him, that his Negroes be treated as children: praised for good work and chastised for bad.

His Negroes, who had become as weary of the wars preceding the final white victory at Dankilizu, were quite willing to settle back and enjoy the peace which had finally come to Dupunu. Those blacks lucky enough to be under the wing of the Pallidins, and that of a few other progressive white families like them, were more

able to enjoy the end of the bloody Settlers War than were blacks taken on by less far-sighted masters. Many white settlers, bitter in losing one or more kin to black slaughter, were prepared to make every black pay— forever and ever, amen. Sean Pallidin, having lost one son when natives had attempted unsuccessfully to burn the early settlement of Mazareenton, swallowed that bitter pill—after a great deal of difficulty—and decided his son was dead, but the living had to make the best of the hand dealt them. While his success wasn't spontaneous, his farm grew steadily while his less perceptive and less adaptable white neighbors eventually sold out, often to him, and returned to Europe.

Once Sean Pallidin had acquired his basic black work force, he very seldom had to go outside his farm to add to it. Like his American counterparts, pre-Civil War, he embraced selective breeding, of his slaves as well as his livestock, which kept his work lists supplied with blacks born and raised on the Pallidin farm. Occasionally, he introduced new blood, but never in any great quantity. Thus, Udu Kujucu and Malba Yuzlu, second cousins, were given permission to breed by Sean Pallidin, the resulting child Sam Kujucu's grandfather.

By the time Sam came into the world, Dupunu had undergone a good deal of social and political change. Even though blacks continued to make up the majority, including the work force, they were no longer slaves. Africa had become a continent in flux, violent rebellions having broken out in the Congo, Rhodesia, and

elsewhere, in efforts, by the blacks, to reclaim their land. While there was an undercurrent of Negro unrest in Dupunu, little of it existed on the Pallidin farm. When all the country's slaves had been freed in an early effort to stem growing Negro dissatisfaction—as well as to postpone any out-and-out war as had occurred in more than one newly emerging African nation—most of those blacks on the Pallidin farm decided to remain where they were; they couldn't imagine more ideal conditions elsewhere.

Chad Pallidin, Sean Pallidin's great grandson, was as perceptive of his times as his great grandfather had been of his. Early, he saw the writing on the wall and knew it was only a matter of time before Dupunu's majority black population would make its move. In preparation, realizing there would be a shortage of blacks to take over the reins of government when the time arrived, Chad set about finding a black man to champion the Pallidin interests. He looked over the black workers on his farm, his purpose to find someone not so potentially brilliant as to be difficult to manipulate, but not so stupid as to fail in the schools to which Chad was prepared to send him. After careful observation of the human "stock" available, and background research that extended to careful examination of the farm's human-breeding books, dating back to Sean Pallidin's time, Chad decided Sam Kujucu was best suited for his purpose, including the boy's age being the same as Chad's youngest son, Phillip.

The plan Chad had in mind couldn't be carried out

in Dupunu where—despite visible advancements of the Negro's bid for equality—there was still segregation in the schools. The whites kept a firm grip on the educational institutions and would have been piqued by any efforts by Chad to raise and educate a black boy along with his own in them.

Chad sent Phillip and Sam to his sister in England, along with detailed instructions on how he wanted Sam's education handled. Melanie Pallidin, by then Lady Melanie Stayte-Browne, had spent most of her early childhood in Dupunu, and she understood exactly what her brother planned. What's more, she heartily approved. While her husband was English, Lady Melanie would always think of Dupunu as her home, and she was willing to do anything to protect her brother's interests there. Under her auspice, her nephew and Sam Kujucu were enrolled in Milton Academy, a prestigious boys' prep school just outside Lincolnshire. It was only Lady Melanie's connections in the peerage that accounted for Sam's admission. Even then, it took her giving him an African pedigree he didn't have. It was as the supposed grandson of nonexistent Chief Basulu Kujucu that Sam attended his twelve years of school abroad. Although he was never completely accepted by his white English classmates, he experienced so little resentment from them that he came genuinely to appreciate their indifference in comparison to that of the Dupunu whites back home.

While it was Chad Pallidin's initial plan to continue Sam's higher (university-level) education in England,

two things changed his mind. One, his son, Phillip, became engaged to an American heiress, Penny Gehenny, in London for "the season". Two, Phillip and Penny decided to immigrate to America, as soon as they were married, to allow Phillip to join Gehenny Oil. Up until then, Phillip had kept Sam in tow and reported, firsthand, regularly, on his progress. Chad didn't feel it wise to turn Sam "loose" in England without Phillip in attendance.

By then, Dupunu had undergone enough additional social and political changes as to have opened its public colleges and universities to "qualified" blacks, as one of many conciliatory moves to pacify its Negroes in their increasing quest for equality. The move, of course, was more show than anything, since few blacks could qualify for admission—their lower-academic educations (in schools where the whites still held fast to segregation) decidedly substandard.

Sam was one of but three Negroes accepted for admission to Deehala University, the public university in Dupunu's capital, and he was one of a total of five blacks accepted for colleges in the whole country. His lack of acceptance by his white Dupunu classmates was soon adopted by black classmates who came to resent his superior and downright arrogant manner.

Needless to say, Sam wasn't pleased with having been returned to Dupunu after spending so much time abroad. If he hadn't felt a debt owed Chad Pallidin, and hadn't realized he'd become a quick nobody in England without Lady Melanie's patronage, he might not have

returned to Dupunu when summoned. He'd had brief thoughts of following Phillip to America, where it was rumored Negroes had little trouble enrolling in Northern universities, but he had no money of his own, save for the small stipend Chad Pallidin gave him.

Sam found the atmosphere at university tenser than in England but was pleasantly surprised when the white students finally decided to ignore him. There were a few minor incidents but surprisingly few, considering Dupunu still hadn't officially accepted universal integration as national policy. Sam's white classmates were possibly just perceptive enough to see the writing on the wall. While the Union of Gumadi had been able to quell any Negro outbreaks and keep its blacks in check, Dupunu hadn't the money, resources, or the police force to follow suit. Unless Dupunu made an all out attempt to avoid direct and bloody white-versus-black confrontations, echoes of the Kenya's Mau Mau, and the infamous Rhodesian slaughters, were feared to erupt on Dupunu's white doorsteps. The white generation, of college age, was more liberal than its parents, and—while certainly resenting being born when white superiority in Dupunu was on its wane—looked upon Sam in school with them as undesirable but inevitable, taking consolation in the obviousness of his fellow blacks not much liking him either.

By the time Sam was a senior, it was apparent to everyone, in or out of politics, that any concessions the white population had made to the blacks weren't nearly enough. James Hamoobisi, son of two illiterate

blacks, made a visible break with the then existing white government and went into hiding in the country's Dwana wilderness area, reportedly forming an army of black insurgents with intent to storm the capital and take it by force.

Everyone, white and black, walked around as if on egg shells. Negotiations took place, almost daily, within the ranks of the white-controlled government, to determine how many more concessions would be needed to stem the tide of rising Negro nationalism. None of the whites were disillusioned enough to think they would be let off easily, but they were determined not to concede one bit more than was absolutely necessary. Whites had reigned supreme in Dupunu for over two-hundred years, and those whites presently in power were anticipating how they would be written up in history if they gave away far more than was necessary.

A peek into the abyss on which everyone in Dupunu teetered was the raid on the Ustadson farm, without warning, by black nationalists; the house burned, the beheaded bodies of father, mother, and two raped daughters left in the front yard upon which wild animals dined. The country's white minority went into shock. So did many of its majority blacks who saw the line drawn in the sand, didn't want to cross it, if it wasn't crossed already, and resented being lumped with the barbarian Mau Maus of Kenya.

Debate continued among politicians in the white Assembly as more realistic farmers erected wire fences

around their homes and sandbagged their bedrooms. Guns were taken out of racks, loaded, and propped beside doors and windows. Grenade screens were put up in children's nurseries. Women continued to get together on Mondays for tennis but followed it with rifle practice on Tuesdays.

The Miltoni families, in a two-car motorcade, left a party at the country club, at seven o'clock one evening. At a crossroads, Ralph Miltoni and his family waved good-bye to the car carrying his brother, Larry, his brother's wife, Cecile, and two daughters, Leticia and Falla. Less than two minutes later, Larry Miltoni and his entire family were killed when their car hit a land mine in the main road.

Sam graduated university but didn't attend commencement exercises. He'd decided to leave Dupunu, as able as the next man to see what was coming, and with no desire to end up one more dead black man killed in some crossfire.

"You've put a lot of money into me," Sam told Chad Pallidin. "Surely, you don't want to see me and it go up in flames when the pot boils over, here."

"But don't you see, Sam, it was because I saw these very times coming that I prepared you for them," Chad reasoned.

In the other room, there was static from the short-wave. A small band of black nationalists had just been reported suspected on the neighboring Henbell farm. Chad's wife went outside to inform the guards around the Pallidin homestead. In the end, it was a false alarm;

Sarah Henbell was always seeing blacks in her bushes.

"I don't understand," Sam responded to Chad. True, in that what possible reason could the man have had in sending Sam to school for any of this?

"There's to be an announcement within the next few days," Chad confided, his tone indicating something shared that was to be kept in the strictest of confidence. "The white-controlled Assembly is going to throw open the polls in a general election."

"I don't believe it!"

"It's true," Chad assured. "They have little choice, really. There's been pressure from the Union of Gumadi to squelch this before it gets out of hand. Gumadi whites are afraid their Negroes will get high on the smell and nearness of our spilled blood."

"Even if there is a general election, where does that put me?"

"A Negro president is inevitable," Chad said. "The Dupunu white minority will, of course, manage to retain key seats in the Assembly, but the President's cabinet will undoubtedly contain blacks. Do you know how many Negroes there are in Dupunu who are qualified to fill a cabinet post?"

"The blacks, here, seem collectively to hate my guts."

"That's possibly true," Chad didn't argue. "However, we have James Hamoobisi's guarantee you'll be given a cabinet position, even if it's a minor one."

"James Hamoobisi, the rebel?"

"Do you doubt he'll be the black to carry any open

election?" Chad asked.

"But he's behind the brutal Mau-Mau-like killings."

"A few of his men merely got carried away, tired of waiting," Chad rationalized. "We were negotiating with him even as the Miltoni and Ustadson incidents occurred. He was as upset as we all were, anxious for a suitable resolution. Everyone's the loser in an out-and-out war, even Hamoobisi enough of a realist to see that."

"What possible good would I be to you, or to anyone else, in some insignificant cabinet position?" Sam asked, frowning. "Hamoobisi and everyone around him have to know I'm anything but sympathetic to their cause."

"Rome wasn't built in a day," Chad reminded. "Why not suffice it to say that plans are in motion in which you play an integral part. If you're offered a position, no matter how minor, I've promised very important people you'll accept. I hope you won't make me out a liar."

"Of course, I'll do what you think is best," Sam said. He was surprised at how quickly he warmed to the idea of holding even a low-totem post in a new government. With potential for what? Sam saw only one governmental position wherein he might give Chad Pallidin the help the white farmer hoped, and that was the Presidency. No matter what kind of manipulation went on behind the scenes, Sam saw no way he could ever get that. His well-known debt and beholden to Chad Pallidin made his election to just about any political

office nigh on to impossible, as long as there remained the black majority.

He looked back on those times and doubted he could have predicted the course of events that followed. Had anyone been able to predict them? Know James Hamoobisi would die of a heart attack? Know Frank Pilusi would become president and not be opposed by whites still holding key positions within in the Assembly? Know Pilusi would choose Sam as his Vice-President? Know Pilusi would perish in a mysterious explosion? Had Chad Pallidin known? Hadn't he told Sam there was a plan in the works in which Sam would play an integral part? Wasn't Sam now in that one position, President, he'd once doubted could ever be his?

Certainly, there had been indications that Chad Pallidin had known something. After Sam joined James Hamoobisi's cabinet, in the predicted insignificant capacity, Pallidin had continued to tell Sam it was only the beginning. Sure enough, with James Hamoobisi's death, Sam found himself Frank Pilusi's Vice-President; although, still with no real power. Pilusi didn't like him, made no secret he'd only appointed him because of the white minority's threats to again throw open the polls: which would have replaced Pilusi as certainly as night was replaced by day.

Then, there was talk of a conspiracy to shoot Pilusi. Chad Pallidin brought up the possibility to Sam, and Sam accepted the idea with ease, surprised by how desperately he'd come to want Pilusi's seat. Not only

did Sam despise the Negro playboy President, who had succeeded James Hamoobisi, but Sam actually believed he'd make a far better president. Also, he wanted to prove to his fellow blacks that he could get to the top without them. The primitive bastards hated him because, with Chad Pallidin's help, Sam had been lucky enough to make something of himself where most of his peers had yet to poke their heads outside of their cow-dung huts. He'd show them their mistake and how he had hitched his fortune to the right star.

As much as he found himself favoring the idea of Pilusi's assassination, he never really saw shooting him as all that feasible. Sam wasn't allowed close enough to him to do the shooting. Besides, the white minority had so easily accepted Pilusi as President, Sam appointed as his Vice-President, that the blacks were nervous and had Sam closely watched. None of them needed a genuine IQ to see what would occur if and when anything happened to their man Pilusi.

Chad Pallidin assured Sam that everything was already all worked out. Trust in Chad, and Sam would find himself King of the Mountain. Hadn't Pallidin been right so far? Besides, it wasn't necessarily for Sam to deliver the fatal bullet. After all, his discovery as part of any assassination conspiracy would have ruined everything.

Did Sam have access to anyone close to Pilusi? No; Pilusi had been quite thorough in weeding out enemies from the small coterie he kept close.

Did Sam know Pilusi was sexually interested in

attractive blonde white women, as evidenced by his having taken Gena Mullen as his lover? So, what if Pilusi hooked up with another such attractive blonde white woman, this one with a gun? In fact, Chad had one in mind—Paula Tarner. If Pilusi's people, who so constantly monitored Sam, were to report back to Pilusi that his Vice President was sleeping with white, blonde Paula, wouldn't the President's curiosity be aroused? Sam, though, thought it highly unlikely, even if Pilusi was curious, that the President would ever have trust in a woman met under such extenuating circumstances.

Besides, why would Pilusi ever involve himself with anyone else as long as Gena Mullen shared his bed?

Chad smiled and said he had it on good authority that Gena Mullen would soon be out of the picture, although not even Chad knew the how or why. It had, though, been suggested to him by people who, up until then, had been very good at getting things right.

Gena not only fled the Presidential Palace but the country. With her exit, Sam had, for the first time, been struck by how deeply the conspiracy to kill Pilusi might go.

He sat back, did whatever was requested of him by Chad Pallidin, and waited, finding himself suddenly thrust into the Presidency not by the expected shooting death of Pilusi but by the totally unsuspected explosion of the Presidential yacht with Pilusi and Paula Tarner on board.

Since then, Sam was convinced he'd been a good President. Naturally leaning in favor of his white

supporters…without whose help he would hardly have made it to where he was…he still didn't believe he'd completely compromised the Negro cause. However, it didn't escape him that he still wasn't trusted by the blacks and was in no way endeared to them. It had, thus, been quite easy for him to stand in the way of various pieces of legislation which the blacks wanted but which the white farmers, like Chad Pallidin, opposed.

There was no doubt in Sam's mind that Pilusi's death had been murder. There was little doubt the white minority was somehow involved.

His suspicions now enabled him to look upon Denim Grady's investigation with some indifference. He doubted Denim would ever uncover anything detrimental to the white faction that had hired him. Sam's ease only increased when Gena Mullen came back to Dupunu as Denim's teammate. However, Sam was surprised and upset when he learned from Chad Pallidin that Denim had uncovered hints of the one-time plot to assassinate Pilusi by gunshot.

"Don't worry about it," Pallidin insisted, laughing over the rim of a glass of whiskey. "There's no smoking gun to tie you directly to any plot, involving bullet or bomb."

"He's asked me for an interview."

"Who?"

"Denim."

"You agreed, of course?"

"Yes."

"Good. You'd only convince him you're somehow

involved if you went around acting like you are."

"What, though, can he possibly want from me?"

"Don't be naïve, Sam," Chad chided. "You've always been someone with a lot to gain from Pilusi's death?"

Chad stood.

"I'd better leave," he said. "We don't want any reports going out that you were closeted with me for an inordinately long time, do we? We might raise suspicions that we're cooking up something."

He went to the door, turning back before he opened it.

"Don't let Denim intimidate you, Sam. There's no possible way he can prove Pilusi was murdered, let alone pin any of us, you included, to it."

"There's never been a perfect crime," Sam reminded.

"Not that we know of, anyway," Pallidin said with a laugh. "Besides, it's never been necessary to have a perfect crime, merely to have all the loose ends properly secured."

# CHAPTER SIX

Denim excused himself and left the Dupunu President.

He got in his car and drove to Gena's apartment, perplexed that the pieces still hadn't yet fallen into place. Everywhere he turned, he came up with nothing but blank walls. Somewhere, somebody had to have answers. A yacht and all the people on board didn't spontaneously combust without some explanation besides an act of God.

"Any luck?" Gena headed to the wet bar to fix Denim a drink.

"*Nada.* Zero. Zilch. The big goose egg."

"Well, I've a bit of good news," she said, bringing Denim his drink and going for hers on a sideboard.

"I doubt I could survive the shock of any good news," Denim said, settling into a chair and slipping off his shoes.

"Our part in the investigation is over," Gena said.

Denim poised his glass at his lips.

"Apparently, Pilusi's death is no longer Classification One," Gena said, settling down with her drink on the couch facing Denim. "It's now Classification Two.

I have little doubt but that in a few months, it'll be even farther down in priority. We have been offered the chance to stay on in some "other capacity"; mercenaries are always of value in country's teetering on the edge, and, a solution to Pilusi's death or not, the blacks aren't going to stand for Sam Kujucu, and his white friends, lording it over them much longer."

"Do you think the blacks will make a move against a constitution they've so recently ratified?"

"What do *you* think?"

"I think the whites have moved ahead in a game incorrectly assumed by some to have a set of fair ground rules," Denim said. "The problem, of course, is that the blacks have never really accepted *any* rules. There's a clash of cultures here. No matter what anyone says, white is not black, nor vice versa. I think the whites are like adults cheating at chess with a mentally deficient child. And when the child gets frustrated and knocks the board to the ground, stomping on it and the pieces, who really wins the game?"

He emptied his glass, stood, and walked to the bar. He'd never been too excited about taking on this job, but he felt cheated in having been freed of it without stumbling upon the answers.

"A solution wouldn't likely have been a real solution, anyway, Denim," Gena consoled, sipping woody-tasting liquor. "It would have only made matters more impossible for everyone involved. It'll be better this way; and, it's not as if we failed. We've merely been taken off the case before we solved it. That's hardly

a black mark on either of our performance records. Maybe things will work out. Maybe the blacks will overcome their collective sense of being screwed and hold out for victory in the long run. Maybe they won't. Maybe there'll be a few more years of compromise. Maybe the killings will erupt on a grand scale tomorrow. No matter what happens, it's unlikely the true story of Frank Pilusi's death is going to be revealed in time to stop any of it."

# EPILOGUE

It was warm, verging on hot and saved from it only by trade winds blowing in off the water. When Gena opened the door, she wore only a small, two-piece orange bikini that did little to conceal her exquisite body, complete with full breasts.

"Denim Grady!" she said, sounding if she didn't believe her eyes; she didn't.

"Hello, Gena Mullen," he said. "May I come in?"

"Jesus, yes, please do!" She moved to let him by. "I heard you'd been killed in the raid at Collumpopo."

"I lived through that, no favor of the marauding blacks," he said. "Do you think I could have a drink?"

"Of course, you can have a drink. Scotch, your preference if I recall?"

She went to the wet bar; Denim sat in a chair.

How quickly the three years passed. It seemed just yesterday the two made love in her hotel room in Dupunu and said good-byes.

Gena seemed little changed. Then, there had been little, during the last three years, to make her change. She'd abandoned Dupunu before all hell broke loose. She hadn't bothered to return, after it had begun, either.

She brought Denim his requested drink and suggested they go out into the sunshine by the pool.

It was a decidedly idyllic setting: the water, the palms, the huge ferns, and the low roar of a man-made waterfall that tumbled into one end of a man-made basin that looked surprisingly natural.

Denim began to relax, recognizing this tranquil setting as the real thing. In Dupunu, the last few years, he couldn't afford to be caught off guard, even in spots like this. At any minute, black savages could come bounding from behind palms and ferns, wielding machetes that would turn the water of any falls, and any pools, to pale pink. There had been just the case at Collumpopo. He shuddered as he recalled the smell of all that spilled blood, mutilated bodies, and nightmarish shrieks as blacks reverted to the primitive.

"You're lucky to be finally out...and alive," Gena said. "From what I hear, the blacks have, now, seized the airport. Every time I picked up a newspaper, and read what was happening there, I thought of you having stayed on...and died."

"You were lucky to get out when you did," Denim said. He took a large swallow of Scotch, wondering if he could get drunk. In Dupunu, he drank to quench his fear but never got to get drunk for fear any debilitating inebriation might well be his last.

"Wasn't I lucky, though," Gena agreed. "You know, I somehow thought, after the last night we spent together, you'd decided to get out of Dupunu, too."

"There always seemed to be something turning up

to stop me." In truth, he just couldn't resist the money he'd been offered to stay on in an advisory capacity.

"Well, at least you're out, now," she said. "As, by the way, is Bagley Tyles who I ran into a couple years ago in Rome. You remember Bagley?"

"Vaguely," Denim admitted.

"He lucked out, too," she said, "and was out of there before the blacks went totally ape-shit."

He had thanked her for having warned him off. Actually, she hadn't remembered giving him any such warning. What had he told her, though, over drinks in the Italian capital?: *I knew you had a nose for survival, Gena. I got out as soon as I heard you did.*

Beyond the pool was an expanse of mowed lawn, then the beach, then an ocean different from the one that lapped the shores of far Dupunu.

"I still haven't adjusted to no longer having constantly to worry about being some black man's target?" Denim said.

"Just how long have you been out?"

"Three months."

"And you haven't looked me up before now?"

"I didn't even know where you'd decided to hole up until I talked to Hamie Gallou in Palm Beach, and he said you'd set up house here."

"He's certainly doing very well for himself, these days, isn't he? Hosts some very big parties, and one of his yacht designs got last year's Denninger Trophy. No one in the States seems to give a rat's ass if there was ever a black man in his family's woodpile. He should

have left Dupunu years ago, instead of waiting around until it was almost too late. You'd never know, though, that a grenade took off his right leg at the knee, would you? Thank God *you* came through unscathed."

"Actually, I've a few new scars, these days, to be sure," Denim said, "but, luckily, nothing vital is missing." He added as a seeming afterthought: "Hamie told me about the bomb, by the way."

"He told me, too," Gena said, although he thought it was something she hadn't known. "We had a good old-fashioned drunk one evening at the Breakers Palm Beach. Strange how simple it was, all said and done, the explosives built right into the ship's superstructure and concealed by all that shielding steel."

"You believed his explanation for bomb going off?" Denim asked.

"By way of a malfunction? You know, as well as I do, from demolitions training, that it's just possible. If it was programmed to detonate by remote control, as Hamie says, it might well have been triggered inadvertently by something as innocent as someone's cellphone call."

"You knew Hamoobisi quite well. Could he have ordered the bomb built into the yacht?"

"Oh, yes! He was well aware that Dupunu's relations with the Union of Gumadi might eventually go sour if blacks were ever permanently to head Dupunu's government. A plan to activate the bomb, after the yacht was given to the leader of Gumadi's white government, was certainly not beyond Hamoobisi's way of

long-range thinking. With the Gumadi leader dead, somewhere up the road, it's conceivable the country's blacks would have taken the opportunity for their long overdue revolt; Gumadi whites blaming the yacht's destruction not on Hamoobisi, who booby-trapped his gift, but, rather, on some local black Gumandi militant group."

"You ever consider it might have been Hamie who detonated the bomb?"

"Hamie?" Gena laughed. "What did he have to gain by blowing up Frank Pilusi?"

"Well, he was having sex with Paula Tarner before she moved on to Pilusi after you'd jumped ship that first time."

"Well, there is that," Gena said. "Maybe he *was* jealous enough to blow up his ex and the man who stole her. Crimes of passion have been committed for far less."

"Except, I don't think he blew up anyone or anything," Denim said and looked into his empty glass. The heat of the day had evaporated the last of its ice. "I don't think Hamoobisi would have told Hamie on what frequency the remote control devise was programmed to detonate the bomb. Hamie wouldn't have had any need to know. If he did do it, why deny it, now, and he does deny it? Who's left to care that any of those people went up in a ball of fire, except, maybe, for me with my innate sense of curiosity?"

"Want another drink?" Gena asked, standing and reaching for Denim's empty. "There are usually a

couple of servants to do these menial chores for me; but, being my generous self, I've given them the afternoon off, my not having expected an old friend to show up at my door."

He didn't give her his glass. He merely rolled it back and forth, back and forth between his opened palms.

"I think *you* blew up the yacht," he said.

"You're serious?" Gena asked after a noticeable pause.

"Why deny it? Who any longer cares? Isn't that what we just decided? Granted, I wouldn't die on the spot without the answer; however, it does remain as frustrating as hell to have spent so much time trying to figure out a puzzle to which you may have always had the missing pieces."

"How and why me?" Gena asked. "What did I have against Frank Pilusi?"

"You're the only one, besides Hamoobisi, who I figure might have had access to information on the frequency to detonate the bomb. Hamoobisi might have told you when he'd never have told Hamie Gallou."

"You think Hamoobisi didn't know I was being paid by the whites who brought me into the picture specifically to watch him and pass on just such pertinent information?"

"The rumor was that Hamoobisi had come to love and trust you."

"Would you like that refill of Scotch, or not?" she pressed.

This time, he surrendered his glass.

She walked back to the house and disappeared into its shadowy interior. She reappeared in a few minutes with drinks, ice, glasses, and more of the same, rolled in front of her on a portable bar.

"It's too long a walk to keep going back and forth to the house," she said, handing Denim his fresh glass. She took her own and returned to the chaise longue she'd vacated but minutes before.

Denim didn't say anything.

Finally, Gena said, "When you and I, the first time, were brought into Dupunu from the Grey Zone, by the white contingent, to negotiate with Hamoobisi on the matter of his assuming the country's first presidency, it was obvious to anyone but a blind man that the man was sexually besotted by me. I was quite prepared to milk it for all it was worth, too. Certainly, I didn't climb into his bed for anything but the money our employers were paying me for information, because I found him physically unattractive. More often than not, I had to think of you, while I was having sex with him, just to make my orgasms seem real. Whether or not it was true love that made him eventually begin to confide more and more in me, especially once I stopped passing on information—which I did merely to put him more at ease and, possibly, get even more valuable information, later—I don't know."

"He told you about the yacht he was having built as a gift for the leader of Gumadi. He told you about the bomb he was having built in it?"

"At first, I didn't realize of what great value that was

to me. But one day, I had the epiphany as to how it could see me into full retirement. While, like every other independent agent—I suspect, even you—I had a sizable nest egg saved up for the day, it was never enough to keep me from accepting the next job and then the next…"

She sipped her drink, a faint smile on her lips.

"I went to some whites I knew in key positions within the Dupunu Assembly and who I knew would do most anything to get back complete control, and I told them, for a price, I'd get them what they wanted."

"You killed Hamoobisi *and* Pilusi?"

"It wasn't as difficult as you might think. Hamoobisi did have a slight heart condition. Therefore, few questioned the diagnosed cardiac arrest as the cause of his death. The blacks assumed that, with Hamoobisi dead, the white minority so obviously disliking Pilusi, that there'd be another general election. Secretly, though, the whites persuaded Pilusi they'd back him if he just appointed white-friendly Sam Kujucu as his Vice-President. By the way, Sam Kujucu wasn't my specific choice. I just guaranteed the vice-president slot *would* be made available and requested my benefactors position *someone* amicable to them when it happened. After Pilusi made it official that Sam Kujucu would be his vice-president, after the whites made it official that they were no longer moving to have another general election, all I had to do was wait for the opportune moment to detonate the explosive and remove Pilusi from the picture."

"And the conspiracy to assassinate Kujucu by shooting?"

"A red herring," Gena admitted. "It was thought best to give everyone without a need to know something to occupy their attention. As for bringing Paula Tarner into the picture at all, I was already more than a little tired of sleeping with Dupunu presidents, by then, and saw the diversion as my way out."

"When the bomb went off, Hamie had to know what it was."

"Certainly, he knew, but if he opened his mouth to say anything, he would have only put his foot in it. As far as he knew, he was the only one left alive who'd known the device existed; the demolition man who installed it had been eliminated by Hamoobisi shortly after the job was done; Hamie, too, would have been killed if Hamoobisi had lived long enough. If it came out Hamie knew, it would follow, by way of logical assumption, that he'd detonated it to kill his ex-lover and the man who stole her. Certainly, no one, not even Hamie, had any evidence to connect me to any of it."

And so the final pieces, for Denim, finally had fallen into place, but what difference did his seeing the final picture really make, now, except for satisfying his curiosity? Sam Kujucu was dead, assassinated by black nationalists. Hamie Gallou was minus half a leg and designing ships. Gena Mullen sat there, healthy, beautiful, tanned, retired, likely very rich and very content, despite her having been responsible for much of what had happened. Or, maybe, she wasn't responsible, in

that it might very well have played out pretty much the very same…except for Gena not getting her nest egg… even without Frank Pilusi's death on the exploding presidential yacht. Maybe it was always inevitable that the blacks would be helplessly compelled to do their bloody thing, all over Africa, like they'd done in the Congo, in Kenya, in Rhodesia, like they were now doing in Dupunu, and as they would probably, eventually, do in Gumadi.

# ABOUT THE AUTHOR

**WILLIAM MALTESE**, the internationally bestselling author of novels, short story collections, and his popular Stud Draqual Mystery Series, has published (under various pseudonyms) close to two hundred books in genres including gay and straight erotica, sci-fi, science-fantasy, mystery, romance, western, adventure, espionage, cooking, wine, and children. With a Business/Advertising degree, Maltese enlisted in the U.S. Army, where he achieved and was honorably discharged at a Sergeant (E-5) rank. Presently, he divides his time between the Pacific Northwest and New York City. You can visit his websites or email him at:

www.williammaltese.com
www.myspace.com/williammaltese
www.facebook.com/williammaltese

email: williammaltese@yahoo.com